# drop

WITHDRAWN

·LISA·
PAPADEMETRIOU

·knopf·
new york

Copyright © 2008 by Lisa Papademetriou

All rights reserved.
Published in the United States by Alfred A. Knopf, an imprint of Random House
Children's Books, a division of Random House, Inc., New York.

Knopf, Borzoi Books, and the colophon are registered
trademarks of Random House, Inc.

Visit us on the Web! www.randomhouse.com/teens

Educators and librarians, for a variety of teaching tools, visit us at
www.randomhouse.com/teachers

*Library of Congress Cataloging-in-Publication Data*
Papademetriou, Lisa.
Drop / Lisa Papademetriou. — 1st ed.
p. cm.
Summary: Sixteen-year-old math prodigy Jerrica discovers she has the ability to predict
outcomes in blackjack and roulette, and joins forces with Sanjay and Kat to develop her
theories while helping them get the money they desperately need.
ISBN 978-0-375-84244-3 (trade) — ISBN 978-0-375-94244-0 (lib. bdg.)
[1. Gambling—Fiction. 2. Probabilities—Fiction. 3. Ability—Fiction. 4. Emotional
problems—Fiction. 5. Family problems—Fiction. 6. Las Vegas (Nev.)—Fiction.] I. Title.
PZ7.P1954Dro 2008
[Fic]—dc22
2008002568

The text of this book is set in 12-point Centaur.

Printed in the United States of America

November 2008

10 9 8 7 6 5 4 3 2 1

First Edition

I can calculate the motions of heavenly bodies,
but not the madness of people.
—Sir Isaac Newton

(Not yet a player?
Peruse the gaming terms on pages 167–169.)

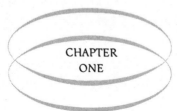

CHAPTER
ONE

i t was a good hand. Two aces: a diamond and a spade. As Sanjay put in three red chips, meeting the bid of the guy next to him, he imagined himself with a real spade, digging up diamonds. *That's why I'm here, isn't it?*

He tapped a fingernail against the crisp edge of the card, waiting for the player across the table—Mark, a guy with shaggy blond hair—to deal the turn. With a soft snap, the card hit the Formica tabletop: ten of hearts. *Damn.*

A short, squat guy with a haircut like a perfect suburban lawn shifted in his seat. Sanjay knew that either he had nothing or, if he had something, had no clue what to do with it. Sanjay prided himself on his ability to read people. It was one of the reasons that he enjoyed dropping in on these college games sometimes. The high school ones got stale after a while.

*Every table has its chump,* Sanjay thought, *and at this table, that chump is Allan.* But with his pristine pink shirt, ironed khakis, and heavy gold watch, maybe Allan didn't care. His type were all over these college games. Betting with Daddy's money. Parents that didn't even notice when a few thousand went missing. Enrolling in Nevada State University when their families couldn't buy their way into the Ivy League.

Mark's thick fingers turned over the next card: ace of hearts.

Sanjay's own heart thrummed, and he felt his pulse racing through his neck. He tried his best not to advertise his excitement like a Strip billboard flashing into the desert night.

Three of a kind. Strong cards. But not . . . unbeatable.

Next card: three of diamonds.

Kristin, a blond girl with a low-cut black shirt, leaned against the table, and Sanjay's blood fizzed a little. A small flutter of her eyelashes told Sanjay that she had something. *Beware of Kristin.*

Mark turned his cards over. Sanjay had been watching him for the past two hours—he was a cautious player whose small stack of chips didn't accurately reflect his skill. Sanjay knew that all the best poker players folded more than they bet. Morons always stayed in too long. That's what made them losers.

Kristin tossed in a red chip. *Not too aggressive.* Her pile of chips told the story. Sometimes girls came to these games because they wanted to meet guys. *This one is here for the money.*

Beside her, a guy who could have been Asian—or Latino?—knocked the table.

"I'll raise," soon-to-be-loser Allan said, and put in two reds.

Sanjay saw his bet, and the guy to his left muttered, "I'm out."

Asiantino guy saw the bet. Then Mark turned over the flop.

Jack of hearts.

Asiantino guy cleared his throat as Kristin put in a blue chip. Her large eyes were a strange color—more yellow than hazel. And unnerving.

Asiantino saw the bet, and so did Allan. The chump still had nothing, and Asiantino had just touched his watch—his tell. In the past two hours, every time this guy tapped his watchband, someone else took the hand.

Some guys gave away when they had something, some gave away when they had nothing, and some never gave anything away at all. *You just have to watch.*

Sanjay put in his blue chip. Time for the river.

Mark lifted the top card. The deck was from the Diamond Horseshoe—the kind you could buy in any cheesy gift store on the Strip. He turned it over, setting it gently on the table. And there it sat, making its silent statement. Ten of clubs.

Three aces, two tens. Full house.

The aces actually felt hot in his fingertips. *Do not think about how good the hand is. Don't think about it.*

His chips were piled in tidy columns before him. Across the table, his eyes met Kristin's.

*I could do some damage,* he thought, just as the Asiantino saw Kristin's two-blue bet. Sanjay didn't have enough chips to take her out completely—he'd lost a few hands—but he could blast a huge hole in her take, then sink her in the next round or two.

"I fold," Allan said. *God, what an idiot,* Sanjay thought. *So obvious from the start that he had nothing—why couldn't he just accept it and get out early?*

Sanjay flipped up his cards, just enough to reassure himself that the red and black *A*'s were still under his thumb.

A quick breath in through the nostrils and Sanjay shoved his palms forward. "All in," he said as the chips trooped toward the center of the table.

"What's up, High School?" Mark asked. "Got a hot hand?"

Sanjay didn't respond. All these college guys liked to rip into him.

"This is getting interesting." Kristin looked down at her cards, tilted back in her chair. Her yellowy eyes shone into his like lights, making him cringe a little. *She has something good—but is it good enough?*

The seconds ticked by on his watch—Sanjay could practically feel the long, slim whisker as it clicked across the face, counting time.

*Bet or fold, bet or fold. I'll win the hand either way*, Sanjay thought, but there was only one way he wanted to win it. With Kristin's money stacked neatly in front of him.

Finally, a quick intake of breath and Kristin laid her cards on the table, facedown. "Fold."

Sanjay felt his heart squeeze with disappointment. *Almost had her*, he thought. *Almost*. He leaned forward and was about to reach for the chips when Asiantino shoved his messy pile forward and nodded at Sanjay's cards. "Let's see them."

Christ, he'd forgotten Asiantino was still in the game. Sloppy. *Well, at least I'll take someone down*, Sanjay thought as he turned over his aces.

"Full house," Mark said, nodding.

Asiantino smiled a little. Then, with the slow deliberateness of a surgeon, he flipped over the two cards in front of him. Queen of hearts. King of hearts. He didn't look up.

Sanjay felt the floor drop away. There was nothing around him but silence.

"Aw, man, a royal flush!" Allan said with an annoying snort laugh. "Man, the cards are really dropping for you, Kal."

Kal—Asiantino—reached for the chips, and Sanjay stood up. But Kal never made eye contact, and that was when Sanjay knew that the tell had been a setup. Or maybe Kal had just been looking at his watch. Maybe Sanjay had read him wrong. This thought was worse than watching his money flow into someone else's hands.

"Rough," Mark said as he handed the deck to Kristin. She gathered the cards and stacked them cleanly. Mark stood up and reached out his hand. Sanjay rose and shook it.

"Well, I guess I'll see you guys some other time, some other game," Sanjay said.

Mark smiled out of one side of his mouth. "Come back when you've saved up some of your allowance."

Sanjay laughed because he was supposed to, and Mark sat back down at the table. Kal watched the cards in Kristin's hand as they danced their familiar shuffle-cut-shuffle step. Sanjay stepped out into the warm night air, letting the door snick closed behind him.

*Too much light pollution in Vegas to see anything at night.* With no stars in the sky above, Sanjay felt cut off from the greater universe. He walked toward his car and climbed in behind the steering wheel.

The engine growled and his headlights lit up the low houses and green lawns along the street. Green, green, green. So green it made your eyes hurt, even in the darkness. *An upper-middle-class oasis in the middle of the goddamn desert.* Sanjay shifted into first and headed for home. *Maybe next time.* Tonight was . . . part of the learning curve. *Next time, for sure.*

\*\*\*

Her right hand was a fist. A headache thrummed at her temples as the dream receded, hazy and indistinct. Around her, white walls reflected the eerie green numbers of her digital alarm: 3:48 a.m. *Still two hours and fifty-seven minutes left before I have to get up,* she thought automatically, waiting patiently for the room to stop spinning. She looked at the bottle of pills on her nightstand, its white label glowing. She had taken the small yellow tablet tonight, which was part of why she was so tired and wired. At night, the medication made her grind her teeth. During the day, it made her feel as if her head was attached to her neck by a strand of spiderweb.

Jerrica tucked her head against the soft white pillowcase and shut her eyes. Like a slow, spreading fog, the dream began to creep back. She had the impression of flower petals. Petals upon petals, locked in a perfect spiral. The petals were mud-brown and blood-red—ugly.

*Just a dream,* she told herself. But she couldn't fight the feeling that the dream held an important meaning. It was there, just at the edge of her grasp . . . then it fluttered away . . .

Jerrica's eyes snapped open, and she flipped on her bedside lamp. Silently, she began to recite a series of numbers. Or, rather, it was one number—pi. Most people thought of it as 3.14. But pi is infinite. A single number, spilling into eternity, without pattern, without repetition.

Jerrica had studied pi in an independent course last semester, and it had quickly replaced her fascination with prime numbers and Fibonacci sequences. She had memorized pi to the first two hundred twenty-five decimal places.

But this time, even as she recited the numbers, a distinct feeling of unease crawled over her body.

There was something about those petals and ugly colors. It was as if reciting the numbers made the dream more vivid. It had a message.

She lay on her back, staring up at the ceiling for a moment, then turned back to face the clock: 3:59.

A prime number. It meant something. Something she was just beginning to pick up on.

*I'll never get back to sleep.*

\*\*\*

Kat had seen the little girl—the one in the pink sundress—before. The girl looked up at her mother with eyes like the sea, wide and dark and bottomless. The mother, lumpy and shapeless in an unflattering velour sweat suit, coaxed her daughter toward the iron gate between the concrete posts. The mother's hair was elaborately curled, pinned into an erupting volcano at the top of her head, and her makeup had all the subtlety of desperation. Kat watched as the six-year-old skipped through the entrance and disappeared.

Overhead, the sky was a brilliant blue, so vividly painful that looking at it felt like biting on tinfoil. The cruel sun sucked the moisture from Kat's skin, from her lips. That was the thing about Nevada. It was the desert. *People aren't supposed to live here,* she thought.

Beside the gate, a guard with a gun watched her from the sliver of shadow cast by the visor on his hat. She knew that he was a man—probably a man with a family; a man with a favorite food, a favorite childhood memory—but she couldn't think of him that way. He held a job that should have been performed by robots. *Human beings shouldn't lock each other up. They shouldn't have that much power.*

*Dear Katharine Phelps . . .*

*Two fat women trickled through the gate, followed by the shuffling steps of an old man in a green baseball cap. An entire family—three children of various ages, an older woman (mother? aunt?)—bobbed toward the entrance like ducks. They were joking with each other and laughing, and Kat wondered briefly if they were lost. They acted more like a group on their way to a day at the beach than to a prison.*

*The guard flicked his eyes back to her, and Kat shifted her weight from one foot to the other. But she didn't move forward.*

*Dear Katharine Phelps,*

*We are writing to inform you that your mother, Julia Phelps, . . .*

Kat ran her eyes over the ropes of razor wire curled like a kinky ribbon along the top ridge of the chain-link fence that surrounded the concrete box. The windows were narrow slits, and she imagined a thousand eyes peering out, staring into the parking lot, waiting.

Outside, the world moved on, shifting and changing without them.

The hot wind blew, whispering as it scraped against the hard edges of razor wire and concrete.

*My mother is in there,* Kat thought.

It had been almost twenty months, and the thought still struck Kat as strange, almost impossible. Her mother was serving time in prison for a hit-and-run, while she and the rest of the world were on the outside, living their lives.

*Dear Katharine Phelps,*
    *We are writing to inform you that your mother, Julia Phelps, is scheduled to appear before the Nevada Board of Parole Commissioners on . . .*

Kat checked her watch. She had to be home in half an hour—Aunt Trish needed the car. Once again, she had hesitated long enough for time to make the decision for her. She yanked the handle on the car door, climbed in, and turned on the ignition. She let the engine warm up for a few moments, then turned on the air-conditioning. She hadn't been stopped for long—the car had barely had time to get hot. Still, the cool air was a relief.

She drove away without a backward glance. *Next time. I'll go see her next time. She's not going anywhere.*

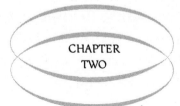

CHAPTER
TWO

"Jerrica, honey, there's something we want to tell you."

The sentence hung there for a moment, like a kite. Jerrica sat perfectly still. *If I don't move, this moment won't bleed on into the next one; the future will stay put, refuse to happen.*

Angela's fingers—delicately manicured, the nails a fragile ballerina pink, with French tips—reached out and wove themselves between Jerrica's father's. His large, square thumb traced the curve between her index finger and her thumb. And Jerrica knew then that the present had begun its steady march toward her.

"It's happy news," Angela said with a hesitant, almost shy smile. The orange flame of the candles was reflected in Angela's dark eyes, two tiny fires. The image of the hideous flower popped into Jerrica's mind.

"You're getting married," Jerrica said so that her father wouldn't have to.

"Yes," Mr. Tyler said. For a brief moment, Angela rested her head on his shoulder, and Jerrica felt as though she had just taken a step off the edge of a tall cliff. The wind whistled past her ears.

The news wasn't unexpected. Look, they had been dating for five years, and Angela had practically been living with them for the past six months. And Jerrica liked Angela—she did. What was there not to like? Angela was smart, beautiful, compassionate—a successful speech therapist. She loved Jerrica's father, and she even seemed to like Jerrica. She had cooked this delicious dinner—this spice-rubbed salmon with mango salsa, these curried green beans, this basmati rice. She even humored Jerrica by placing them evenly apart on Jerrica's plate. *It isn't unexpected.* She inhaled, exhaled. *It isn't unexpected.* "Congratulations," she said.

"There's more," Angela said, reaching across the glossy dark wood table for Jerrica's hand. Now they were joined, like three paper dolls.

Jerrica's father cleared his throat and looked away for a moment. Then his green eyes met Jerrica's. He was a tall man, well muscled, with a head of blond hair streaked with gray. "If you're doing your job, being a lawyer should turn your hair white," he always said when he came home late, his briefcase filled with files. Andrew Tyler practiced a kind of law that Jerrica barely understood, involving developers and real estate.

*I'm nothing like him,* Jerrica thought as she looked at her father, still vigorous at forty-five. Jerrica was sixteen, but she already felt ancient. Fossilized.

Jerrica's hair was dark and straight, almost black, and she was small. There was something about her that made people assume that she was much older than sixteen. Everyone who saw her with her father commented that they looked as different as two people can get—except for their matching eyes.

"Jerrica, you're going to be a sister," her father said.

Silence closed in at the edges of Jerrica's ears and her father's face grew blurry. The mud-and-blood-colored flower hung at the edge of her mind. *Tell them that you're happy for them*, she commanded herself. Her lips tried to form the words, quivered, gave up.

"Sweetheart, of course you have a lot of feelings about this," Angela said. "Of course. But we're going to be a family. This is happy news." There was an edge of desperation to her plea.

Jerrica nodded, but a hot tear spilled over the edge of her lower eyelid. It skated across her cheek and dripped onto her plate. *Stop it. Now.*

"Do you want to talk about it . . . ," her father began as Angela looked up into his face.

Jerrica shook her head. "You just surprised me," she said. *Stop crying.* And she did. After years of practice, this was one thing she could do. *Deep breath in. Deep breath out.* "I'm so happy for you," Jerrica said at last. "For all of us."

She extricated her hand from Angela's manicured fingers and picked up her fork.

"This salmon is delicious, Angela," Jerrica said as she took a bite.

After dinner, Jerrica worked on her homework for a while, then retreated to her room. She had pulled a pack of cards from her bedside table. Now she looked at the irregular pattern of cards spread out before her. Patience. Her mother had always called it Patience. Her father called it Fascination. For Jerrica, it was just solitaire.

Picking up a card from the stockpile, she placed it on the eight of clubs. The red seven of diamonds gleamed up at her as she reached for the next card. It was only when the new card was in Jerrica's fingers that she realized she had placed the seven instinctively, without looking at it.

*Or maybe I just don't remember looking?*

Jerrica held up a card, studying the swirly red pattern on its back. Ovals made of ovals, interconnecting and endlessly repeating. Fifty-two pieces of mass-produced geometry.

The card was light, the tiniest weight against her fingertips.

She closed her eyes and the colors shifted behind her lids. There was a slight falling sensation as the colors swirled and then, like a kaleidoscope, settled into place. The shape—it reminded her of the flower in her dream, but it wasn't the same. The colors gave her a feeling, one she could almost name . . .

*Three of clubs?* But when she turned over the card, it was a nine of hearts. She placed it on the black ten of spades, then rearranged her seven of diamonds and eight of clubs on top of them and flipped over the next card.

Three of clubs.

*There you are. Just a bit . . . late.* The three moved to a four, which moved to a five; then things lined up, and all of a sudden Jerrica was looking at three long tails running from ace to two, and one that stopped at the three of clubs. Only the two of diamonds remained missing.

She touched the top of the stockpile, discarded the first card, and flipped over the next. *Game over.*

Jerrica stared out her window into the dusky light. Next door, her middle-aged neighbor was chatting on the phone in the kitchen, smoking a cigarette and drinking tea. The woman's husband was in the living room, watching the flickering television. Once, Jerrica had heard her father say that the neighbors hadn't spoken a word to each other since their son went away to college. That was four years ago.

*But they must have,* Jerrica thought. *Pass the salt, can I have a glass of water, you're standing on my foot, the phone's for you, I can't believe you're watching that stupid show*—something.

She thought about her three of clubs. How sometimes things can drop into place and the game will start to click. And how, at other times, things refuse to fall into place.

The difference? One card.

One card at the right moment.

Jerrica gathered her cards, shuffled them, and put them back into the box. The box was placed on her nightstand, the edges lined up with those of the table. She straightened the photograph of her mother and climbed between her soft cotton sheets.

*One card*, Jerrica thought, studying her mother's face. *Things can drop right or fall wrong.* In the photo, Jerrica's mother was gazing down at a small newborn—Jerrica's sister, Isabel. They had both been dead for almost seven years. Sometimes, Jerrica sat in the blankness of her room and tried hard to remember their faces. If it wasn't for the photo, she wasn't sure she could manage it.

White walls. There were no other photos or posters—white bureau, white desk, white sheets, white comforter. She had white shelves, but she didn't use them. She could never decide whether to arrange her books alphabetically by author or by title, so they were piled against the far wall in precarious stacks. Her father said that it looked like she'd just moved in or maybe was in the process of moving out, but Jerrica liked the void of her white room. It looked clean. And it meant that the room was never quite dark. The white picked up the green luminescence of her clock radio, creating a permanent twilight.

She closed her eyes, and now the colors behind her lids were darker—green and muddy gray lit with red. There was something about their shapes that unnerved her. A slithering sense of dread snaked around her gut. Her hand clenched as she remembered the dream from the night before. *What did it mean?*

*And why do I keep thinking that it has to mean something?*

*Don't think about it. Don't.* Instead, she refocused her thoughts on how the cards had snapped into place so perfectly. Jerrica tried to remember the last time she couldn't finish a game of solitaire. She had played three games every night before bed for years . . . and she used to lose fairly often. But lately . . .

The cards had been falling for her.

*Enjoy it while it lasts. It'll end. Everything does.*

\*\*\*

Sanjay's father had a checklist for closing the store taped to the side of the cash register, but Sanjay didn't need to consult it. He had been closing by himself for the past eight months—ever since his sister started college—and the list was tattooed on Sanjay's brain.

Lock the front door, straighten the shelves, sweep and mop, zero out the receipts, count up the money, fill out the deposit slip, put the money into the deposit bag. *Time to lock it up*, he thought as he closed the safe. Mr. Patel would take it to the bank the next day. *Sleep tight, money.*

*I hope you don't miss your little friends,* Sanjay thought as he placed a tidy stack of bills into a white envelope. Of course he would return the slight shortage. But he needed this cash now to pay off the minimum on his credit card. Online gambling had racked up some serious damage there. But Sanjay knew that once he got ahead again, everything would get paid off. No problem. He had always caught up.

At least that was one thing he didn't have to explain: his father had co-signed for the card months ago, and Sanjay always paid the minimum balance online. No bills came to the house.

The crisp paper was smooth against his fingertips as he folded the envelope in half, placed it in the pocket of his jacket, and turned to go.

"Oh! Jeez, Ma!" Sanjay stumbled backward a couple of steps and forced a laugh. "Ami, you nearly made me jump out of my skin. How long have you been standing there?"

Sanjay's mother stood perfectly still in the doorway, not smiling. Her eyes were black as stone, and they bored into his, pinning him in his place. "Sanjay?"

He considered lying, but her glance told him that she knew.

"Mom . . . Ami, look." Sanjay walked toward her and took her hands in his. Her fingers were tense, and slightly rough. "I know this looks bad, but I'm just borrowing this money. Abu will never know it's gone."

His mother looked doubtful. "Why didn't you just ask your father for the money?"

"Oh, right."

Her black lashes dipped as she looked at the floor. She nodded her head. It was a tiny movement, almost imperceptible.

"You know this is easier. I'm going to make more money with this . . . loan, and it'll be back in the safe before Abu even knows it's gone." Sanjay knew that his father only compared the total store receipts to the amount in the bank account once a month—when the statement arrived. Sanjay always deposited the checks, but he could float the cash for a couple of weeks.

His mother's features started working—a question forced her straight brows together and the edges of her mouth into a frown. "Have you done this before?"

"Yes," Sanjay admitted. "Twice. I paid it all back, and Abu has never missed the money. Never." *Twice doesn't sound so bad. Better than the truth.*

His mother's eyes traced a line down to his pocket, where the money waited in its fat little fold. "But what if you don't get it back?"

Sanjay released his mother's hands and gave her a gentle kiss on the cheek. "Don't worry," he murmured. "I'll get it back."

*And more. More, more, more.*

***

Kat's eyes snapped open the moment the door cracked an inch. Her drowsiness evaporated instantly. She felt taut, like a crossbow ready to fire. The light was out in the hallway, but the sliver between the door and the frame was wide enough to let in a faint, silvery glow. Hazy twilight crept in, and cold fingers of fear squeezed Kat's heart. She could barely breathe.

"Kat?" The uncertain whisper fluttered into the room like a pale moth seeking light.

Air trickled into Kat's lungs, enough for her to choke out, "Lala?"

In response, the door opened and soft feet padded across the carpet toward Kat's bed. The light was dim, but Kat could still see her sister's black hair and dark eyes.

Relief made Kat dizzy. She moved over in her tiny bed, making room for Lala to climb in beside her. She lay on her side, facing her sister so that she could feel Lala's breath on her face.

"Nightmare?" Kat asked.

Lala nodded.

"It's okay," Kat said. It was warm under the blanket now that her sister was there, but Kat didn't move, didn't complain. She felt safer, too, somehow.

Lala used to do the same thing when they lived on the other side of town with Julia. Sometimes their mother would disappear for days at a time. And then Kat would have to scramble to find something for them to eat from the bare cupboards. Tuna on pasta. Baked potato with barbecue sauce. Frozen peas and nothing else. Then at night, with the house making strange, uncertain creaking noises around them, Kat and Lala would huddle together under the covers in their mother's bed. Next door, the neighbor's vicious one-eyed black Doberman would bark and lunge, straining at the metal chain attached to a stake in the middle of the yard, until it finally settled down sometime after midnight. It was a mean dog, and Kat didn't like to walk past it on her way to the school bus every morning. But at night, she felt it was a sort of guardian angel, protecting them by its proximity.

During those nights when Julia had disappeared—lost on one of her gambling jags—Kat would lie awake, watching Lala sleep. Kat didn't remember much about her middle school years. Teachers' names and faces were blanks and voids. Her shelves were lined with paperbacks she was certain she had read, although she could not recall a single story. She could remember the gnawing ache in her chest, the blood that pounded through her veins like acid during those years.

Once during seventh grade, while she was crossing the street, a car stopped just inches from her. She had been sleepwalking through her classes. There were dark circles under her eyes like purple bruises—and when she stepped off the curb, she looked right but not left and did not see the car. The brakes squealed, and the smell of hot rubber wafted over her as she stood there, not three inches from the bumper. Adrenaline shot through Kat's body, and she felt a moment of absolute terror. She was amazed at how familiar that feeling was.

Through the windshield, Kat could see the woman behind the

wheel. Slightly older than her mother, pale eyes rimmed with too much eyeliner. She didn't yell at Kat, or hit the horn, or even move. She simply sat there, with her mouth poised in a surprised purple-lipstick O.

Somehow Kat found it comforting to know that this woman, this perfect stranger, was feeling the same fear that she was. They had connected.

Kat turned onto her back to look up at the blank ceiling.

Their aunt Trish's apartment was nicer than Julia's old house, and Trish never spent the night away from them. In the time that Kat had lived with her aunt, the tightness in her chest had begun to loosen, like a shoelace knot that has been picked at and picked at by a patient child. But the hurt was still there.

Kat was still trapped in her mother's sticky shit.

Stiffness crept up Kat's neck. Lala had managed to plant her skull right in the middle of Kat's pillow, and Kat's head was tilted at an awkward angle.

Kat studied the clean lines of her sister's profile. She looked like Julia. Then again, so did Kat—even though Kat and Lala didn't look alike at all. Both daughters were a perfect blend of their mother and her first and fourth husbands, Kat's and Lala's fathers.

Julia looked like a California cover girl—blue eyes, straight blond hair, tall, slim, and gorgeous.

Kat's father was a guy Julia met while she was waitressing at a joint near an army base. Kat had only seen pictures—Anthony was dark as bittersweet chocolate, with full lips and intense, almost shocking hazel eyes. Kat had gotten his eyes, and her hair was a weird hybrid of her parents'—wiry, curly, and honey-colored. Kat was shorter than her mother and much curvier, but she had her mother's facial bone structure. Their smiles were exactly the same.

Lala's father was from Bali. His name was Wayan and he carved furniture for a living. Lala didn't remember him, but Kat did. He was very quiet, and he would let Kat help him sometimes while he was working. He was a really nice guy, so—naturally—Julia ran him off pretty quick.

Lala's mouth was half open, her breath even. She muttered something in her sleep.

"Are you okay?" Kat whispered, but her sister didn't say anything else. Her eyelids fluttered; then she was still.

It was easy to forget that Lala was only ten. She seemed so much older sometimes.

*We both do,* Kat thought. Sometimes she wondered if Lala felt as ancient as she did. An old soul that had been reincarnated too many times into low, difficult lives.

She wondered if Lala felt the same tension in her chest, the same acid in her blood. *But why wouldn't she?* Lala wasn't stupid. She knew that their mother would be coming home eventually. And she knew that Kat would be graduating in a little over a year. Kat imagined that Lala knew fear as well as she did, if not the burden of responsibility.

*Let her hog the pillow,* Kat thought.

***

"The interesting thing about black holes"—Mr. Argent smiled his lopsided smile and paused long enough to brush his fingers through the hair that grew in wispy, fernlike patches across his scalp—"is that they exert a gravitational force so strong that even light can't escape." He tucked the long piece of white chalk he'd been holding behind his ear like a pencil and leaned against the desk, his smile still hanging dreamily on his lips.

Mr. Argent was the physics teacher and faculty advisor to the Rocket Club. Sometimes Jerrica imagined him at home, reading the latest issue of *Scientific American* or *Popular Mechanics.* She didn't know anything about his life, not really, but she felt it had to be something like frozen burritos for dinner, an unmade bed, and reheated coffee for breakfast. It was an image that made her sad—viscerally sad, with an ache in her chest—in spite of the fact that she had no real reason to believe it was true.

*Don't feel sorry for him,* Jerrica told herself. *You're the one who played fourteen games of online solitaire last night.*

After six games of solitaire with real cards, Jerrica had begun to wonder whether she was predicting the cards because she unconsciously recognized them. Maybe marks on the backs—too small to be registered by the eye—were helping her.

So she switched to online games. But, well . . .

Well, she'd been able to predict those cards, too. Not perfectly. But lately the geometric shapes had been appearing in her mind more and more often. She would feel the strange drop in her stomach and then catch a glimpse of the colors and shapes. And Jerrica had begun to realize that the patterns in her mind corresponded with numbers. Yellow and orange with a pattern like a blossom at the center? Ten. Ten of spades, more specifically, because a slight shift with a streak of orange at the center was ten of clubs. Two of diamonds was a neon-pink swirl interlaced with deep sea-green; five of hearts was orange and gold, like a sunburst . . .

"Hey, Sergeant Argent!" called a voice from the back of the room. It was Jimmy Franks, the red-haired third baseman on the undefeated William Henry Harrison High School team. Jimmy was the kind of guy who would put a traffic cone on his head and dance around, singing in a high falsetto. Jerrica had actually seen him do that once, at Emily Waters's party. Jerrica hadn't laughed until he accidentally danced into a coffee table and landed a face-plant into Sarah Mosington's chest, which had recently been augmented as a sixteenth-birthday present from her more-money-than-brains parents. "Hey—if I had a spaceship," Jimmy said now, "and I got caught in a black hole, could I end up on an Earth-like planet on which monkeys ruled over people, only to discover that the planet was actually Earth itself, thousands of years in the future?"

Jerrica sighed. This was Jimmy's usual tactic—to try to send the class careening off course in the hope that he could distract Mr. Argent from any effort at actual teaching.

The class laughed in a knee-jerk way, but Mr. Argent pursed his lips, as though he was thinking it over. "Well, you *could*," he said. "Do you know this equation?" Forgetting about the chalk behind his ear, he picked up another piece and wrote $E = mc^2$ on the blackboard. Then he tucked the chalk behind his other ear.

"Sure—that's Einstein," Jimmy said.

"I meant, Do you know what it means?" Mr. Argent said.

Jimmy gave it a shot. "Energy equals . . ."

Mr. Argent knew better than to wait for the rest of the answer. "Mass times the speed of light squared," the teacher finished for him. "Okay, so the speed of light is constant. What this is saying is that energy and mass are really different forms of the same thing. Look, if you got into a spaceship and traveled three years at the speed of light, many, many years on Earth would have passed in your absence. That's the kind of time travel that could really happen."

"Like Rumpelstiltskin!" This was from Tigger, one of Jimmy's best friends.

Jimmy punched him on the shoulder. "You mean Rip van Winkle, you moron. But could you go *back* in time?"

"No. Time always flows in a forward direction."

"Why?"

Something about the soft, velvety voice made Jerrica turn in her seat.

Mr. Argent's eyes flicked to the far wall, by the back door. "Is that a serious question from Sanjay Patel?"

Sanjay leaned back in his chair and stuck his long legs out in front of him. He was wearing dark jeans and a soft brown suede jacket. "Do you have a serious answer?"

"The serious answer is that nobody knows why." Mr. Argent picked up a piece of chalk and then put it down again. "Actually, some people think that time's flow might be circular. You have the big bang; the universe starts to expand; the universe reaches maximum expansion and begins to contract again until it reaches a mass so dense that—bang!"

The class had fallen silent. Jerrica could hear the wall clock's steady heartbeat ticking. *Why does the second hand sweep to the right and not the left?*

"If it does move in a circle, would that mean that . . . that things are predictable?" Jerrica asked, thinking about the shifting kaleidoscope and the cards . . . five of diamonds, three of clubs . . .

"Well . . ." Mr. Argent hesitated. "You could make an argument, in the abstract—"

"I'm gonna figure out the circle!" Jimmy called from the back row. "Then I'm gonna make a killing in the stock market!"

The class chorused laughter. Even Mr. Argent broke into a smile.

"But could you?" Jerrica asked.

Mr. Argent lifted his eyebrows at her, waving at the class to be silent. "I'm sorry?"

"Could you predict things?" Jerrica asked.

"Well, not the stock market—"

Jerrica cut him off. "What about numerical things?"

"Do you have something in mind, Ms. Tyler?" Mr. Argent pulled the chalk from behind one ear and placed it in the front pocket of his button-down shirt.

"I don't know. Games. Cards, maybe?"

"Cards?" Mr. Argent cocked his head. "Not exactly. If you have a good grip on probability, you can increase your chances of knowing what card will appear when, but you can't *predict* them. But you know that, right? Didn't you study probability last year?"

"Hey, Jerrica, what number am I thinking of?" Jimmy shouted.

Turning, Jerrica saw a pair of black eyes locked onto her face. Sanjay wasn't laughing.

He was looking at her, and something about his eyes made Jerrica itch. *He's noticed me.*

j errica speared a pea with one tine of her fork. The mini-globes were an unappetizing shade of greenish gray cast in the same institutional palette as the sickly pink plastic tray on which they were nestled, but Jerrica didn't mind. For one thing, the colors reminded her of the eight of spades, a card that left her with a happy feeling. Besides that, at lunch nobody bothered her; nobody expected her to talk and make cheerful conversation. She could just eat and read or listen to her music and tune out the world.

A large hand the color of wheat toast reached into her frame of vision and removed a carrot from her tray. When she looked up, Sanjay was smiling at her from across the table. Her heart beat a warning signal as he motioned for her to unplug herself.

She pulled the white buds from her ears.

"You're not eating your carrots," he said, taking another and swirling it into the small tub of ranch dressing.

"I only eat one thing at a time. Carrots last."

"Interesting," he said, and he sounded like he actually meant it. "So—is Argent full of shit, or what?"

"What do you mean?"

Sanjay shifted in his chair. "Do we live in a time circle?"

"Jimmy just wanted to get him off topic."

"You seemed interested."

"I don't know . . . I mean . . ." Jerrica raked her dark hair away from her face. "Have you ever had the feeling of déjà vu? As if you've lived through something before?"

"Everyone has that." Sanjay picked up another carrot stick and held it like a cigarette.

"Maybe."

Sanjay leaned forward, eyeing her sharply. "Jerrica . . . ," he said. "I'm interested."

That actually made Jerrica laugh. Leaning back in her chair, she folded her arms across her chest. "In what?"

"I don't know. In you. In what you're thinking." He smiled slightly. "In something a little more than probability."

"What makes you think I'm thinking of anything more . . . interesting?"

"It's written all over your face."

"I'm that easy to read?"

Sanjay glanced down at the table for a moment before meeting her eyes. "Most people are." He said it almost as though he were sorry, and there was something in his tone of voice that shot through Jerrica like a bullet.

"It seems like . . . well, lately I've been able to predict some things," she said. When Sanjay's eyebrows shot up in surprise, she hurried to add, "Nothing important—just cards." She waited a moment to see if he would laugh.

He didn't.

"Just—when I'm playing solitaire, I know what the next card

will be." She wanted to add *I know it sounds crazy*, but she kept quiet and waited for his reaction.

His glance at her face was searching, and then he seemed to make a decision. Reaching into the breast pocket of his suede jacket, he pulled out the deck of cards. He split it, then pulled out a card. "What am I looking at?"

"I have no idea. It doesn't work that way. It just happens sometimes . . . when I'm in the flow."

"Just guess."

"I don't know. Nine of diamonds."

Sanjay shook his head, flipped over the card. Two of clubs.

Jerrica was unfazed. "I told you that it doesn't work that way. Not for me."

"Okay, so you need to be in the flow." Slipping the card back into the deck, Sanjay shuffled twice, then split the deck with one hand. "Ever play War?"

"Ever been eight years old?" Jerrica shot back.

Sanjay just laughed and dealt the cards forward, back, forward, back, until the deck was finished. "The thing about War is that there is absolutely no skill involved. It's all luck, pure and simple."

"Pure and simple," Jerrica repeated, and for the first time, the phrase struck her as strange. As far as Jerrica was concerned, nothing in this world was ever pure or simple—especially not luck.

They each turned over the top card from their piles. Sanjay had a three; Jerrica, a five. She took both cards. Then Sanjay flipped over a queen to Jerrica's seven; he took them. They settled into the rhythm of the game. Hit, hit, take. Hit, hit, take.

When two jacks hit the table, Jerrica put down her top three cards—four, ten, ace. She felt the slight drop, almost as if she had tripped, as Sanjay lay down his—nine, three, eight. A pattern flashed before her eyes . . .

Sanjay paused, watching her hands, holding a card to his chin. "You think you know what I've got?"

Jerrica blinked, looked at the pile again.

Sanjay had only put down two.

"What am I holding?" he asked.

When she closed her eyes, the colors reappeared. "An eight of spades." She opened them again.

Sanjay flipped over the card. Black eight—spades. Sanjay tossed his eight onto the table and leaned back in his chair. His long legs stuck out beneath the table. *You take up more space than you ought to,* Jerrica thought.

"So—what does it mean?"

"I have no idea."

"But—" Sanjay tilted his head to look up into her eyes. "But you think it means something." When Jerrica didn't reply, he added, "You're a math genius, right?"

Jerrica felt a blush bloom across her cheekbones. "I've taken a couple of college courses." She met his eyes then. "If I tell you something, do you promise not to think I'm insane?"

"No."

Jerrica sighed and leaned back in her chair. "Well, that was honest."

"I try not to lie," Sanjay said.

It was the most comforting thing Jerrica had heard anyone say in a long time. "All right," she said. "Here's the deal—sometimes, when I stop concentrating, stop thinking, I get this weird sensation. Like I'm falling. Just a little drop, as if I've just missed the last step in a staircase. And then it's like—like I'm seeing a pattern ... and the pattern *is* the number on the card ..."

Sanjay gave her a long look. "Ever play poker?" he asked suddenly.

Jerrica shrugged. "My grandfather taught me," she admitted. "We used to play for pennies."

Sanjay interlaced his hands and touched both index fingers to his lips. His dark gaze was steady. Jerrica read a question in his gaze, but she wasn't sure what it was. "There are a couple of guys I want you to meet," he said.

"Hey." Looking up, Jerrica saw a beautiful girl standing behind Sanjay. She was wearing form-fitting jeans and a zip-up hoodie with wide stripes. Her curly blond hair was pulled back into a high ponytail that enhanced the almond shape of her eyes. Jerrica knew who she was—Kat Phelps. "I've been looking for you," Kat said to Sanjay.

"I was just chatting with Jerrica," Sanjay replied, as if there were nothing at all unusual about spending time with someone he hardly knew. He twisted his face up to look into Kat's. "Do you guys know each other? Jerrica, this is Kat."

"Nice to meet you," Jerrica said.

"Same." Kat placed a possessive hand on Sanjay's shoulder and frowned slightly.

*Please,* she wanted to say to Kat, *you're the guy magnet. I'm just the borderline invisible goth girl.*

"Jay, are you coming?" Kat asked. "Stu and Stacy have been asking where you are."

"Sure," Sanjay said. His eyes lingered on Jerrica's, and she felt herself blush slightly. "See you around, Jerrica."

"See you," Jerrica said softly as Sanjay and Kat disappeared into the cafeteria scenery. Looking over, Jerrica spotted Nina Sands and Marty Gwin watching her. Marty leaned toward Nina and whispered something in her ear. Nina cracked up.

Jerrica's eyes dropped back to her tray, but a small smile hovered on her lips. *One of the best-looking guys at Harrison High spent ten minutes talking to me and suddenly I'm grist for the gossip mill,* she thought.

Who would've predicted that?

\*\*\*

Jerrica tapped her eraser against the paper. She looked around to make sure that she wasn't bothering anyone, but the library was practically deserted. It was fourth period, and Jerrica was the only student with an independent study at that hour.

Jerrica had completed Harrison High's senior-level honors calculus class in her sophomore year. Last summer she had taken a math class at the local university, and this year Harrison's principal, Moira Edwards, had given her special permission to study on her own. She had to show her work to Ms. Bligh, who taught AP calculus, every three weeks, but aside from that, all she had to do was produce a proof or paper at the end of the term to collect her credit.

Jerrica stared at the proof she had been working on. It was interesting . . . or, rather, it *had* been when she chose it. But now the more she tried to focus her mind on the problem, the more thoughts of cards and kaleidoscopes and Sanjay crept in.

She wondered how much Ms. Bligh knew about probability. Jerrica was certain that she must know plenty, but the mental image of Ms. Bligh's frowning face and droopy gray eyes was enough to tell Jerrica that it would be pointless to ask her about the patterns and the cards. Ms. Bligh wouldn't be able to grasp the significance.

*Who else can I ask?* Jerrica wondered. Her heart tripped slightly at the thought of Sanjay. He was intrigued by number patterns, too. *And he doesn't seem to think I'm crazy.*

She was certain now that the geometric shapes corresponded to numbers. She just didn't know how . . . or why.

There was only one person who could help her with a question that big.

Quickly, before she had time to think, she pulled her cell phone from her bag and punched in the number.

Professor Watkins picked up after the second ring. "Jerrica, darling! What a delight to see you on my caller ID."

Jerrica smiled at the sound of his clipped voice, the familiar dry humor. "Hello, Professor."

"Now, my dear, please tell me that you are calling with a fascinating mathematical problem, because I've had the most dreadfully dull day."

Jerrica laughed. "Well, actually—I am."

"How wonderful!"

"I think," Jerrica amended. Quickly, Jerrica explained about the cards, about her predictions. "Do you think it's possible that there is a—pattern? To the numbers?"

"A pattern? No."

Jerrica felt a flash of disappointment. But the professor added, "Jerrica, I do believe that there may be a formula—or perhaps a series of formulas—that would help us understand probability better than we do now. In fact, there was a set of principles I was working on in my younger days." She heard the sound of rustling papers at the other end, a friendly static crackle that told her the professor was searching through the piles on his overloaded desk. "I didn't get very far with it, but I could show you what I've got—"

"And you think the principles are showing up in the cards?"

"I think you might be intuiting them, yes. That happens, you see. We have a sense that something is happening, then we have a sense of why it happens, and then we find the numbers to express it. Think about savants—no one understands how their minds work. They make incredibly complex mathematical calculations without ever having been taught formulas—they simply feel their way through the numbers."

"But why would I be able to predict cards?" Jerrica asked.

"My dear, I don't think that you *are* predicting cards." The professor's voice was gentler than usual. "I think you're calculating odds and coming up with outcomes. After all, how do you think probability was discovered? It's all inspired by questions about gambling. In the seventeenth century the Chevalier de Méré—quite a gambler—decided that he wanted to solve this problem: Imagine that two players are betting on a game. They agree to continue playing until one has won six rounds."

"All right."

"Yet they stop after Player X has won five rounds and Player Y three. Well . . ." The professor paused dramatically. "How should you divide the stakes? That question is the entire basis of probability! It's more likely for one player to walk away the winner than the other, but *how much more likely*? The Chevalier asked the brilliant French mathematician Blaise Pascal to answer the question. *And he did.*"

"Amazing," Jerrica said.

"Yes." Professor Watkins's voice was slow and thoughtful. "Of course, shortly thereafter Pascal went completely insane," he added cheerfully.

"What?"

"Well, he underwent some sort of mystical experience," the professor explained. "He left everything—not only money and possessions, mind you, but friends as well—and went to live in a monastery in Paris. He spent his time working on a book called *Pensées.* It was all about God and religion and whatnot. And then, of course, there was Pascal's wager."

"What's that?"

"Oh, a very famous fragment of the book—two pages he wrote by hand, the handwriting going every which way. Part of it read, 'God is, or he is not. Which way should we incline? Reason cannot answer.'" The professor's voice dropped to a pensive growl. "Almost as if he had moved beyond mere probability."

Jerrica wished that she could see the professor's face—she could imagine his bushy white eyebrows fluttering toward the middle of his forehead, the way they did when he was excited about a new idea. She could almost see the sparkle in his blue eyes, the rapid dancing of his fingers as they tapped across the desk, impatient and eager to get his ideas on paper, quick, quick!

"Beyond probability," Jerrica said, and suddenly something surfaced in her mind. She caught a glimpse of it before it slipped back into the water. "As if he had found meaning in the numbers? A pattern . . . or equation? Do you think—"

"Do I think that he may have found a way to plumb the depths of the human experience through numbers?" Professor Watkins finished the thought for her. "Do I think that he found the Answer?" His voice turned deep, mock-serious. "My dear Jerrica, I have no idea. I cannot hope to psychoanalyze someone who lived hundreds of years ago."

"No, of course not," Jerrica said quickly, but her heart was racing. It was the same feeling that she got when she played cards—

the feeling that she was at the tip of a mystery and that she could solve it, if only she had enough time.

Everything was pointing in one direction—forward. "Professor," she said, "if I work on this problem—could I call you sometimes? To get some feedback?"

"Well, my dear—what, exactly, would you say the problem is?"

"I want to see if I can quantify the equations," Jerrica explained. "If I can turn my intuitions"—she didn't want to say "visions"—"into math."

"I see . . . Well, my dear girl, I'd be delighted to help you," the professor said. "It would be a wonderful break from these cement-headed students they've been feeding me here. Honestly, this is one of the most interesting questions I've heard in a long time. And it could have profound implications. Profound." Professor Watkins cleared his throat. "I'd be happy to show you my work on the subject . . . if you're interested."

"Oh, I'm interested," Jerrica told him. She was surprised at the passion in her own voice. "I'm very, very interested." *And I think Sanjay Patel will be, too.*

\*\*\*

A car horn bleated as Sanjay accelerated through the turn. He was on his way to Jerrica's neighborhood, a wealthy, manicured part of Vegas with the kind of perfect green lawns that would have been impossible without irrigation, chemicals, and cheap immigrant labor.

His parents' argument was still broadcasting in his ears, loud enough to drown out the angsty pop that was playing on the radio.

"I can't go to the henna ceremony without a gift," his mother had said. "It'll look like we don't have any money."

"We bought a gift for the engagement party. We will give a gift at the wedding. We can't give a gift at every function—it's absurd," Abu shot back.

"It's expected." Ami's voice was brittle. "And it's expected that we will help with some of the expenses—"

"Don't ask me for that! None of your relatives helped with *our* wedding—"

Sanjay had been standing in the kitchen, listening. He couldn't see them, but he could picture his father lying back in his brown faux-leather recliner, his feet up, showing off a hole in the toe of his right sock. His mother would be standing beside the coffee table—the one she had rescued from a tag sale and repainted yellow with bright red poppies. Their ranch house was small and crammed with his mother's repainted treasures. She had attended design school in India and had a gift for painting. But once Sanjay's parents had moved to the United States, his father had insisted that she give up her work to help out at the store.

"I find it *interesting* that you care so much about what other people think." Sanjay's father had made the word "interesting" sound more like "disgusting."

"Those other people are my family. Of course I care what they think." Sanjay had been surprised at the iron in his mother's words.

"Do you care what your husband thinks?"

Ami didn't rise to the bait. "I will not go to the function if I don't have a gift," she said. "I will simply call and tell them that I won't be able to attend."

"Then that's your choice."

Ami retreated upstairs to make her phone call, and Sanjay walked out the back door to the car, fighting the bitterness rising in his throat. *Dad just doesn't get it. He thinks we can live as if other people's perceptions don't matter. But perception is everything.*

If Ami's family thought she was cheap, then that was what she became—in her own eyes as well as theirs. It made him sick to think about it. Sanjay would have loved to step in and save the day, but . . .

He'd managed to pull ahead a little, but he still needed to come up with nine hundred dollars by the end of the week so the store receipts and the bank statement would match.

Sanjay pulled up in front of Jerrica's house, taking a moment to admire it. The large Colonial and the beautifully landscaped yard were completely out of place in the desert. Sanjay guessed that the house had been built within the past eight years. Who knew? His uncle may have been the builder. It was the kind of development Uncle Raj favored—a well-planned, elegant neighborhood in an excellent school district.

*There is a reason my father doesn't live here,* Sanjay thought as he stepped out of the car and onto the smooth black pavement. *It's because he doesn't understand that the way people see you controls reality.*

***

Sanjay and Jerrica barely spoke as he guided his father's car from her residential neighborhood to another gated community halfway across town.

It was seven o'clock, and Jerrica's father thought that she was on her way to the library to study. He had seemed so happy when Sanjay came to the door that Jerrica had almost felt proud, as if he were a gift for her father. Mr. Tyler gave her a huge grin, then clapped Sanjay on the shoulder with a wide hand. As they walked out the door, Jerrica almost forgot she wasn't on a date. And they definitely weren't going to the library.

Sanjay waved to the security guard in the booth, and after a few moments, he drove up to a monstrosity—a hideous redbrick behemoth with fat white pillars in the front and a second-floor balcony. *The house looks like it was designed by someone with a seriously short attention span,* Jerrica thought as they made their way up the front walk. The landscaping consisted of scrawny, immature trees and shrubs that seemed to be struggling out of the earth. In Vegas, Jerrica knew, anyone with money could build pretty much whatever they wanted.

"Ready?" Sanjay asked. His index finger hovered slightly over the doorbell, like a moon eclipsing the ghostly pale glow that leaked onto the dim porch.

"Do I look okay?" Jerrica asked, surprised as the words kicked from her lips like a reflex. *I never say stuff like that.*

Sanjay smiled. "Why do girls always ask that?"

"I have no idea. Forget I asked."

"Forgotten," Sanjay said.

Jerrica nodded at the heavy oak door, which was topped with an overwrought piece of leaded glass cut in a pattern to look like a rising sun. *Or maybe a setting sun?*

"Let's go in," Sanjay said.

She hesitated.

"You look fine," Sanjay said.

"Whatever." But her heart was fluttering.

Sanjay rang the doorbell. A moment later there were footsteps, and just before the door opened he leaned toward her. She felt the warmth of his breath on her ear as he whispered, "Actually, you look great." Immediately the door whooshed open and Bo Cravens stood there, his pale hair wild around his face. When he saw Sanjay, his face broke into a grin. "Hey, man!" Bo said warmly. "Haven't seen you in a while!"

"It's a Thursday night in Vegas." Sanjay held up a fist, and the two guys knocked fists. "Show me the cards."

Bo laughed. "Everyone's in the back." His blue eyes drifted to Jerrica, then back to Sanjay. "No Kat tonight?" he asked.

Sanjay shook his head. "My girl hates cards, man. Hey—do you know Jerrica Tyler?"

Bo shook his head. "Nope, I've never had the pleasure—"

"We're both in Sellers's Modern Euro," Jerrica said, overlapping his words. Instantly, she felt like an idiot. *I sit three desks behind him,* Jerrica thought. She hadn't realized that she was quite that invisible.

But Bo played along. "Oh, right!" he said quickly. "Sure, Jerrica. Hey, come on in, you guys."

The house was filled with the comforting smell of chicken soup. Bo led Jerrica and Sanjay past a stiff-looking living room full of faux antiques and into a brightly lit dining room. Three guys were seated at a dark wood table beneath a showy crystal chandelier.

Jerrica was momentarily mesmerized by the rainbow of light coming from the crystal. A teardrop blinked blue fire at her, then red. *Internal light refraction,* Jerrica thought, amazed at the cut glass's ability to radiate the entire color spectrum.

Sanjay sat down in a plush taupe dining chair. "Dudes," he said.

"Yo, Jay." Antonio Mendez looked up from the deck he was shuffling. "Good to see you, man." His dark eyes took in Jerrica, then swept back to his cards.

Jerrica hovered uncomfortably at the edge of the table for a moment, wishing she could escape or just disappear. But Sanjay's eyes flicked to the chair across from his own. Hesitantly, she sat down and placed her palms on the glossy wood surface of the table.

"What's up, Jay?" asked a good-looking guy Jerrica knew was named Nguyen. He had spiky black hair and wore a button-down blue-checked shirt and a black V-necked sweater. Nguyen was one of the few guys at school who had serious style. "What's up, Ms. Tyler?"

A small thrill shot through her at the sound of her name. Nguyen was a year older than her and had been in her honors math class during sophomore year, before she started taking college classes over the summer. *Guess I'm not completely invisible.*

The other guy—Goose—just nodded at them and kept quiet. Although she had never been to a game, Jerrica knew that Goose was on the football team. With his thick neck and short haircut, he was the kind of guy others habitually called Big Guy.

Nguyen shuffled, and started dealing.

Sanjay shrugged out of his jacket and slung it over the back of his chair. "What are we playing?"

"Texas Hold 'Em," Goose said.

Sanjay nodded in approval and reached for his wallet.

"Did Sanjay tell you how we do this?" Bo asked as a card skimmed over the table and landed in front of Jerrica. "Everyone buys fifty dollars' worth of chips. Keeps it easy. When you're out, you're out, but we don't usually play until there's only one winner."

"Not on Thursday anyway," Antonio said as he tossed in the blind.

"Minimum raise is a dollar," Nguyen said. "And we do double blinds."

Jerrica nodded, reaching into her bag for the money. She

folded almost immediately in the first couple of rounds, barely even glancing at the cards that landed in her hands. Instead, she watched the cards as they came up in the turn, the flop, the river. Sanjay won the first pot—a little over ten dollars—and folded early in the next two rounds.

With the next hand, Jerrica found herself looking at a ten of hearts and a ten of spades. Three cards were spread across the table before her: a jack of diamonds, a two of spades, a four of clubs. She stayed in. Goose reached for the top card, and she felt her breath lighten. The room spun—a merry-go-round, a twirling top, a clock; the colors were twisting, taking shape, stopping before her eyes—and she knew before his fingertips touched the deck that the flop would be a ten of diamonds.

She shook her head, recovering, blinking at the card on the table.

Ten of diamonds.

Nguyen folded, and so did Sanjay. Bo tossed in two chips, and Jerrica matched him.

"Hell, I might as well stay in," Goose said as he shoved two red chips toward the center.

Goose turned over the river: four of diamonds.

Jerrica stayed in.

"Let's see what you've got, then," Bo said, lifting his eyebrows at her bid.

With a graceful move, she revealed her three of a kind.

Bo frowned. "Nice," he said.

"I'm out." Goose dumped his cards on the table, and Jerrica reached for the chips.

"Hold on a minute, chief," Bo said, turning over his cards. "I've got a full house."

Jerrica stared. There they were—he had been holding a four and a two. It wasn't a mistake.

He lifted his hands. "Sorry," he said.

"Oh, no problem," Jerrica said quickly, shoving the chips in his direction. "Guess I got a little too eager."

Looking up, she saw that Sanjay was watching her closely. Jerrica felt her cheeks burn. *What happened?* she thought as Antonio took another turn as dealer. She'd seen the ten coming, but she hadn't been able to read Bo's hand.

She folded in the next two rounds, then finally won a hand. She predicted one or two cards before they appeared, but she couldn't seem to get into the flow. It was like a river traveling too quickly to drop a boat into. Sanjay hadn't even glanced in her direction for the past twenty minutes. She shifted in her plush chair, increasingly uncomfortable.

"Well, guys," Sanjay said finally, checking his watch. "Looks like I've got to jet."

"What?" Nguyen protested. "We haven't taken all of your money!"

"I always leave while I'm ahead," Sanjay replied as Bo cashed out the fifty-two bucks' worth of chips he had left. "But maybe you'll get lucky next time."

Bo handed Jerrica her cash—thirty-seven dollars. "See you guys tomorrow," he said.

*Did he mean me, too?* she wondered.

"Later," Sanjay called as he took Jerrica's elbow to lead her to the front door. Goose waved, but Antonio was already dealing the next hand. Nguyen was looking at his cards. Jerrica was enjoying the warm pressure of Sanjay's fingers on her arm. She felt as if they were locked together, two links in a chain.

Sanjay pulled the door closed behind them, and then they were alone on the front step. A shiver ran through Jerrica as she remembered what Sanjay had whispered before they stepped inside.

For a moment, neither of them spoke. "Well, that didn't go quite the way I'd hoped," he said at last, shoving his hands into the pockets of his jacket.

"I'm sorry." Jerrica shook her head. *Stupid,* she thought to herself. *Stupid to think that I could ever make math out of a card game...* "Sometimes I could see the cards, but—"

Sanjay's eyes were reading her face, as though he expected to find a novel there. "But?" he prompted her.

"But not always. I...Sometimes I felt as if I could tell what cards were going to come into play. But I couldn't see what the other players had."

"Okay." He put his hand on her arm again, and Jerrica felt a small wave of pleasure. Sanjay's manners made it easy to pretend she was on a date with him.

"Come on," Sanjay said as he led her down the walk toward the car. "I'll take you home."

*But I don't want to go home.* She wanted to head back inside, to figure out what was happening with the cards. *But it's late, and Dad will be worried about me.*

She wanted to ask Sanjay if he would ever talk to her again, but somehow the question felt childish, so she kept quiet. Overhead, an orange streetlamp buzzed. Then Sanjay's car gave a chirp and the front lights blinked yellow. He opened the door for her.

"Thank you, Sanjay," Jerrica said softly as she stepped into the car.

"Not at all." Sanjay waited until she was settled before closing the door.

A cold weight settled over Jerrica, as if a heavy piece of marble were weighing her down. She shifted in her seat, unable to get comfortable. Now that she had lost, Sanjay wouldn't care about her anymore. *He was interested . . .* , she thought. For a moment, they'd shared something—a mystery. *But now he doesn't believe in me.*

CHAPTER
FOUR

"Is it just me," Kat hissed through her smile as she toyed with her wineglass, half full of brilliant red cranberry juice, "or is everyone here ignoring me?"

Sanjay sighed as he scanned the roomful of his relatives, chatting and laughing. "It's nothing personal. They ignore my entire family. We're the poor relations."

Kat's right eyebrow lifted, and Sanjay found himself admiring its smooth curve. He wanted to run his thumb over it, but knew that it would cause some family drama if anyone noticed. "My uncle has some serious money," he said.

"Obviously," Kat said, looking around the room. This was the fanciest party she had ever been to.

Sanjay's uncle Raj had moved to Vegas at the beginning of the building boom. His company had built several upscale developments on the edge of town, thus enabling him to throw his daughter this lavish engagement party in a fancy hotel and to fly the groom's entire family to Las Vegas for the event. Sanjay surveyed the scene—tables piled high with food, a four-foot ice sculpture in the shape of a swan, purple table linens that matched the flowers flown in from Central America that very morning . . . All very grand and very tacky and very expensive. *Very Vegas.* But what Sanjay respected most about his uncle was that even if he didn't have the money, he would have found a way to throw the same party. Everything he did, he went all in.

Kat set her glass down and bit into a crisp dumpling. *"Mmm."* Steam curled from the edge as the flaky pastry crumbled over her lips. "What is this?"

"Samosa," Sanjay said. "Try the sauce," he added, spooning a small amount of green liquid onto her plate. "Careful—it's hot."

Kat dipped a corner of her samosa into the sauce and took another bite. Her eyes lit up, which made Sanjay smile.

"I love your cousin's outfit," Kat said as her eyes lit on Rinku. She was wearing a light green beaded shalwar kameez—a long tunic worn over loose pajama-style bottoms. "And her jewelry is amazing." Filigree gold dangled from Rinku's delicate ears, and a slender gold chain was pinned into her black hair along her perfect part. A gold pendant dipped onto her forehead, shimmering with tiny diamonds.

"It's very traditional."

"Everyone's clothes are so colorful!" Kat gushed. "I feel like a lump."

"You look fantastic," Sanjay told her. Of course, she did stick out in this swirl of brilliant kameezes, ghararas, and saris in her sleeveless black dress and tall black boots. But she looked good. Very stylish. "Do you want to get some air?" he asked suddenly.

"I think I could use some."

Outside, it was soft and quiet as they walked down the manicured path that embraced the enormous hotel. Cube lights lit the jasmine-lined walkway. The simple outdoor scene was a relief from the giant chandeliers and blazing lights of the party. Kat sucked in a deep breath.

"How's your mom?" Sanjay asked after a while.

Kat thought for a moment before answering. "She's up for parole."

"Ah," Sanjay said.

"Yeah."

"How do you feel about that?"

Kat shrugged. "I don't know," she said, hedging. Kat had never filled Sanjay in on her mother's complete history, but he knew the essentials. "Not too thrilled, I guess."

"So . . ." Sanjay turned to look at her. Her golden hair was backlit by a streetlamp, which gave her a sort of halo. "What are you going to do about it?"

"Do?" The question caught Kat off guard.

She was about to ask him what he meant when Sanjay let out a sigh. He was looking beyond her, at a bank of tall grasses that provided a privacy screen for the pool.

"Hello?" She touched his shoulder gently and Sanjay looked down at her, his eyes coming into focus, as if they were adjusting to a sudden change in light.

"Kat—" Sanjay's voice was soft. He wished he could tell her everything—about how he had fallen behind again, how he had taken money from the store. But he knew she wouldn't like it.

If only his father had joined his brother-in-law's business instead of opening his own. No doubt it had been what his mother was thinking when she suggested they move to Vegas. Sanjay was certain that she hadn't envisioned a life working at a small ethnic grocery store.

"Yes?" Kat said.

Sanjay bent toward her, cupping her face in his hands.

She lifted her chin and he kissed her throat, then her collar-bone. Kat felt a familiar thrill shoot through her body. His hand ran down her spine, to the small of her back . . .

A cough split the night, and Sanjay took a step backward. Kat's head was still spinning from the kiss as she turned to see a stocky man in an ill-fitting business suit. He had Sanjay's dark eyes and black hair, but that was where the resemblance ended.

"Abu." Reflexively, Sanjay took a step away from Kat, feeling the heat rise to his face, glad for the darkness. His father didn't approve of public displays of affection—actually, he didn't seem to approve of affection at all. Disapproval was stamped on his face. The silence grew thicker and more awkward until Sanjay finally said, "Kat—I believe you've met my father."

"Hello, Mr. Patel," Kat said. She looked at Sanjay uncertainly.

"Hello." Mr. Patel replied without even glancing her way. "Sanjay, I believe some of our relatives are looking for you."

"Yes." Sanjay nodded. "Of course. We were just heading back."

He didn't take Kat's hand as he started back toward the brilliant lobby. Kat felt stung as he turned his back on her. She risked a quick glance at Mr. Patel, who was gazing at his son's retreating figure with a strange mix of disgust and pride.

\*\*\*

"How do you feel about that?"

The words hung over Jerrica like a claw. As if she were inside one of those arcade games, the kind with the stuffed animals and cheap watches settled limply at the bottom of a glass box. Overhead, a silver claw would drop down and thrash at the toys, slicing through them in an attempt to grab one, pull it out of its comfortable nest, shoot it through a tube and into the world . . .

"What should I say?" Jerrica asked, attempting a dodge. "So my future stepmother is having a baby . . . How am I supposed to feel?"

Jerrica's therapist, Janet Mayfair, had a habit of pulling out Claw Questions just when Jerrica was least expecting them. They had been coasting for weeks now, with Jerrica sitting on the sage-green chenille couch, describing the minutiae of her life. Today she was having trouble concentrating on what Janet had to say. Her mind was still buzzing with her most recent conversation with Professor Watkins, earlier that day.

"I can't tell you that." Janet looked at her through fashionably rectangular glasses. She had short silver hair and always wore tailored pantsuits. To Jerrica, she looked as if she lived a secret life as a bank executive. What a contrast to the funky fabric art that hung on her walls, the lush green plants in every corner and on every surface of the office, the tiny statue that sat on her desk—a knot of dark wood the size of a child's fist that was meant to represent a Buddha in prayer.

Jerrica looked out the window at an unromantic view: the black roof of the building next door and a rust-orange water tower in the distance. "I remember when Isabel was born."

"She didn't live long."

Jerrica looked at Janet sharply, but the therapist didn't flinch or shift in her seat. "It seemed like a long time," Jerrica said.

Janet nodded. "Yes," she said slowly. "I'm sorry. Yes. Three years can be a very long time when someone is sick."

"It was."

"Do you have any memories of your life before Isabel?"

Jerrica thought for a moment. She remembered how drawn her mother's face became after Isabel was born, how irritable she always was. She would go off at any moment. As if she were a gun, cocked and ready to fire. Jerrica remembered trying to be invisible, noiseless, without any needs. Her mother had changed. She was different after the baby came. Isabel's illnesses—infection after infection in her lungs—were taking a toll. But what was Jerrica supposed to do? Drop off the face of the earth? She was constantly terrified that she would say or do the wrong thing. *My memories before Isabel? I remember an orange. A flight of stairs with red carpet.* "No," she said at last. "No memories."

"But you were seven when she was born."

Jerrica just nodded.

"Jerrica, how do you really feel about Angela having a baby?"

"Babies need a lot of attention," Jerrica admitted. She pictured Isabel when she first came home. Her tiny closed eyes; her protruding lower lip, wet and as ripe-looking as a plum. From the moment she'd arrived, Isabel quickly became the center of her parents' world. The constant illnesses, the frantic phone calls to the doctor, the trips to the hospital. Sometimes, before she fell asleep, Jerrica imagined that she could still hear the hiss and rattle of Isabel's breathing as she struggled for air. It had been the sound track to her life for three lonely years.

Jerrica looked up at the art over Janet's shoulder, a small quilt in a brown wooden frame. The quilt was a medallion in the shape of a six-pointed star. The star was made of hundreds of tiny equilateral parallelograms, beginning with yellow at the center and working through orange and into vibrant red at the edges. It was a beautiful exercise in precise geometry, an expression of one end of the light spectrum. It reminded Jerrica of the number five. "You know what? I don't want to talk about this."

Janet's delicate nostrils quivered as she inhaled deeply. "Okay," she said, tracing a finger across the smooth gray wool that covered her knee. "What would you like to talk about?"

Suddenly Jerrica's heart felt like a blown egg—hollow and frag-ile. The dream had appeared again ten days ago, and she'd had it al-most every night since then. Each time, she woke with nothing but a vague sense of dread and an intricate pattern of muddy red. If the pattern corresponded to a number, she didn't know what it was. "Do you think that things happen for a reason?" she said at last.

"Do you think that they do?"

"I don't know." Jerrica's stomach twisted uncomfortably. "Some things, maybe."

"Did you have something in mind?"

"No—it's just . . . I met this guy. It's not anything romantic, nothing—"Tension crept into Jerrica's temples. *Nothing romantic?* An image of Sanjay's beautiful skin, full lower lip, thick black hair . . . then the room tilted and she forged ahead. "It's just—it's funny that I met him now. I mean, we're both interested in the same things, and the timing is just . . ."

Janet supplied the word: "Synchronicity."

"Yes."

"Is it comforting for you to think that the universe might have a plan?" Janet asked.

"In some ways," Jerrica admitted. Although in other ways, it made the world seem like a cruel place.

Janet regarded her. She was waiting for Jerrica to say something more.

The small white room stayed silent.

In the quiet, Jerrica heard the professor's words from earlier that day. "Jerrica," he had said, "you can't control everything."

She had told him—in hypothetical terms, of course—about Bo's poker game. "My dear, poker is useless when it comes to probability," Professor Watkins had insisted. "There are too many variables! What cards are in the players' hands? Are they bluffing? Are they overly cautious? Do they even understand the true probability behind winning? One is bound to get caught up in psychology, and it's like I always say, my dear: psychology creates nothing but chaos."

"Psychology creates chaos," Jerrica murmured.

Janet tipped forward at her waist, trying to catch the words. "Sorry?"

Now Jerrica glanced at the small black clock on the low wooden table beside Janet's nubby cream-colored wing chair. "We're out of time," she said.

Janet didn't look at the clock. "True," she said. "But I think we should stay with this a little longer."

Jerrica looked down at her nails. The tips were short; half of her black nail polish had chipped away. She felt disheveled in this pristine, sunny office. Like a grubby caterpillar that couldn't blend in with its surroundings.

"All right," Janet said at last. "I'll see you next Thursday."

"No . . . we're going to be out of town then." The words spilled out of her mouth, unplanned.

"Really? Your father didn't mention it." Janet picked up her square black notebook—she still used a paper calendar.

"It's just for two days. Dad has to go to Reno for business. Angela and I are both going along." It was a strange little lie, but an easy one. Her head was light with the freedom she had just given herself. A Thursday afternoon, all hers. Perhaps she could talk to Sanjay. Maybe they could try again at a different game.

Yes, maybe that would make all the difference. Time to find out.

## CHAPTER
## FIVE

Jerrica spotted Sanjay on his way to school. He was walking through the parking lot with Kat and two guys Jerrica didn't know. She hesitated, almost shrinking behind the tall potted cypress at a corner of the rear entrance.

Kat said something that made Sanjay laugh. Jerrica felt almost caught up in the laugh—it pulled her forward. "Sanjay?"

He turned, tilting his head a little, a smile still lingering on his lips. "Jerrica," he said, with only a slight edge of wariness in his voice.

"Can I talk to you for a minute?" Jerrica asked, feeling extremely self-conscious as she hitched her messenger bag higher on her shoulder. It was nearly empty and kept sliding down her arm.

Sanjay shrugged. "Sure."

Jerrica felt her face burn. She couldn't—wouldn't—say anything in front of the others, especially Kat. They'd think she was crazy.

After a beat, Sanjay understood. He turned to his friends. "Hey, guys, I'll catch you later, okay?"

The two guys—Jerrica knew that they were seniors but didn't know their names—looked at Sanjay. One of them punched him in the arm and said, "Later, man."

Kat folded her arms across her chest and lifted an eyebrow.

Sanjay tugged one of Kat's golden curls and released it. "Go ahead," he said. "I'll catch up with you."

Kat was wearing a pair of cropped cargo pants and an Empire-waisted pink shirt that made her café au lait skin look rosy. *What would it be like to be so beautiful?* Jerrica wondered. Kat flashed her a look—narrow-eyed and suspicious—and then flounced away. Once she was gone, Jerrica felt like she could breathe again.

Sunlight glinted off the glass door as it swung shut behind Kat. Sanjay waited until it was fully closed before he turned his face to look at Jerrica. "So," he said. "What's up?"

She took a moment to bask in his glance. There was a warm, spicy scent that radiated from him, but Jerrica wasn't sure whether it was cologne or simply the unique smell of his skin. "Look, I don't know exactly what happened at the poker game, but I've been thinking about it and I think there were too many variables." Jerrica's words came in a rush. "Too many players. Too many hands."

Sanjay pursed his lips slightly, as if he knew this already and didn't see the relevance. "Right."

"It mixes up the probability," Jerrica explained. "I need a game that's more controlled."

"Well, maybe we can go around challenging second graders to games of War." Sanjay smiled indulgently, the way you would at a small child who was being very silly but didn't realize it. "Could be a real moneymaker." He turned away, as if the discussion were over. Jerrica felt as if she had been thrown overboard or tossed into a well—the sudden fear when Sanjay turned his back made her instinctively want to flail desperately and reach for a rope.

"I was thinking of twenty-one," Jerrica called.

That made Sanjay stop. Slowly, he turned to face her. "Blackjack."

"You really only have to worry about two hands—yours and the dealer's," Jerrica explained. She felt the rope in her hands, taut, pulling her toward . . . something . . .

Sanjay ran a hand through his black hair. "You want to hit a casino?"

Jerrica took a deep breath. "I think we should."

"Do you have a fake ID?"

"Oh. No."

Sanjay nodded. He looked like he was considering something carefully. "Well," he said at last, "I can get you one."

***

"No." Kat slammed her locker closed with such force that the metallic clang vibrated through Sanjay's chest.

"Oh, come on." Sanjay trailed after her as she made her way through the crowd of students milling toward homeroom. Being in school always made Sanjay feel like he was in an ant farm—disturbingly unimportant. "It's no big deal."

"Not for *you*," Kat snapped, and kept on walking. "There are about a thousand people who could get you a fake ID, Sanjay."

"Yeah—and they'll look about as real as a showgirl's chest." The ants crawled past, and Sanjay thought about how little he would care if a giant shoe crashed through the ceiling of the school. *Who are these people?* he wondered. The crowd that swarmed around him—he couldn't pick any of them out of a lineup.

Kat tugged on a curl, extending it to twice its usual length. "I'm not calling him."

"You said that you guys were on good terms nowadays," Sanjay said.

"We are—I just . . ." Kat's voice trailed off. Lately she'd heard some things about her ex-boyfriend that she didn't like. True, Mike had always been a little dangerous—he'd dropped out of high school, had been in and out of juvenile hall three times, and made a tidy side income selling fake IDs that were totally convincing, down to the holograms. But the new rumor was that he was using, maybe dealing. He was a piece of her past that had followed her to this new school last year, before she'd realized how completely she could make over her life. She had dated him until last October, when she'd met Sanjay. Sanjay, with his immaculate clothes and elegant manners. With his enviably normal family. Sanjay was not only smart but analytical, a planner. Mike could never see more than ten minutes into the future, just like her mother.

She stopped three feet outside the door to her homeroom and leaned against the wall, hugging her books. "I don't want to just call him and ask for a favor."

"It's not a favor if we're paying for it," Sanjay protested. Normally, he would have let the subject drop. But the guy who supplied Sanjay's ID had vanished. And there was something about that Jerrica . . . something that intrigued him. He couldn't help feeling that her weird-sounding probability theories held some nugget of truth. "You'd be just another customer."

"Then *you* do it."

Sanjay laughed. Mike had punched him in the face once—the third time Sanjay and Kat had hung out together. "Hey"—Sanjay jammed a fist into his pocket—"what are you doing Saturday night?"

Kat looked at him doubtfully. "Why?"

"I thought we could go out. Somewhere nice." Batting his eye-lashes, he put his palm against the wall behind Kat and grinned right into her face. He was so close that she could smell the mint of his toothpaste, feel the heat from his lips.

She lifted her eyes to meet his, felt her body responding to his presence. "Okay," she said.

"Good." Leaning forward, Sanjay gave her a soft peck on the lips. "It's a date."

"A date?" Kat asked, and smiled as Sanjay laughed.

"So—what do you say, Kat?" he asked. "About the other thing?"

Kat sighed. "Fine," she said.

"For real? You'll call him?"

"I'll call him," Kat said, and then—just as the bell rang—she turned and walked into the classroom. Ms. Evans hadn't arrived yet. Not unusual. She was always late to homeroom.

"Lay-tah, sexy mama!" Sanjay called after her.

Kat gave him the finger over her shoulder and the class cracked up.

Sanjay trotted off down the hall, toward his class. He was late for class again, and Mrs. Andrews wasn't like Ms. Evans—she was right on time, like a hip-hop beat, which meant that Sanjay would have to spend an hour after school in detention.

*Who cares?* he thought. *Blackjack and Jerrica Tyler. It has possibilities. Lovely possibilities.*

\*\*\*

One week later . . .

"The usual?" Sanjay asked as Mr. Murgai brought three pack-ages of phratas to the counter.

"Of course." Mr. Murgai's sleepy eyes crinkled at the edges as he smiled, leaving deep marks at either side of his nose. The old man came in every Wednesday to buy the same thing: a bag of almonds, a bag of cashews, three packages of phratas, a few jars of premade sauce, and a few dates. If he ran out of garam masala, he would buy some of that as well. He was a bread-and-butter customer—the kind Sanjay's family counted on to support their business.

"Are you being a good son?" he asked in a voice loud enough for Sanjay's father to hear. Mr. Patel looked up from his inventory clipboard, but did not smile.

Sanjay laughed as he rang up the sale. "Of course, Mr. Murgai. Are you being a good husband?"

"Of course!" the man boomed. "Just don't ask my wife." He helped Sanjay pack up the bags, grinning as he carried them out of the store. Then he disappeared as the door swung shut with a jingle.

Sanjay stared after him for a moment, then glanced at his father, who had turned his attention back to his work. "Did you see what he bought?" Sanjay asked his father.

"Phratas, almonds, cashews." Mr. Patel touched a can with the end of his pen and made a note on his clipboard.

"And that horrible curry sauce." Sanjay leaned against the counter. "Mom makes much better sauce. We could bottle that ourselves, print up some labels, sell it under our house brand . . ."

A frustrated snort shot from his father's nostrils. "People like to buy brands they know."

"If they shop here, they know *us*. We're the brand."

Abu moved on to the next row. Sanjay knew what that meant—case closed. But he couldn't let it go. "*We're* a brand, Abu," Sanjay said. "Patel Grocery. People buy from *us*."

"It's a big project, Sanjay," his father countered. "Do you really want your mother slaving away in the kitchen? It isn't easy to start a business. Believe me, I know!"

"I'll help. I'll—"

"You?" Mr. Patel laughed, then nodded, then shook his head. "You? You've got school to worry about." He made another note.

"But this could make a lot of money. If it takes off, we could sell the stuff at other stores under our brand—"

His father's face clouded. His arm dropped to his side, and—for the first time that afternoon—Sanjay got the sense that he had his father's undivided attention. "You need to care about school, and that's all. You need an education. Work hard—that's the way to succeed in this country. Look at Priya."

Sanjay's sister was studying accounting at the state college. He knew that his parents wanted a respectable profession for him, too. Doctor would be ideal, but engineer would be acceptable. "The way to succeed in this country is to have ideas," Sanjay said.

"Well, you have plenty of those," his father scoffed.

"And some of them have paid off," Sanjay pointed out. He gestured to the candy racks he'd insisted his father add near the cash register. Abu had said that they were tacky, but now most customers grabbed a halvah bar or a bag of chocolate-covered almonds on their way out.

The glare he got from his father would have been enough to stop most people in their tracks. "There is more to life than money," his father snapped. "You need an education." He turned his back to Sanjay and walked through the office door.

Sanjay cursed quietly to himself as he grabbed a towel and wiped off the counter. He was so sick of this little store, this little life. It was as if his father had bought into the idea of being the hardworking immigrant, grateful for his tiny piece of the American dream. But Sanjay knew that the universe had a different plan for him. A bigger plan, a bigger life. More, more, more.

If he won.

A good hand at the right time. The right card, the right roll. If Jerrica could help even a little, things could turn around for him—fast. Maybe she could count into the decks and figure out when a high card was going to come up. That would give them an edge. He'd heard that there were people who could do that.

It was a small hope to cling to, a piece of flotsam in a wide ocean. Sanjay held on tight.

The bell over the door jingled and Sanjay looked up into the warm, dark face of David Raj, the store's weekend night manager. He had smooth, dark skin that reminded Sanjay of the shell of a hazelnut.

"Hey, David."

"Everything okay?"

Sanjay just sighed and looked over his shoulder, nodding toward the office.

David smiled ruefully. "Ah," he said. He knew all about the tension between Mr. Patel and his son. David placed a hand on Sanjay's shoulder. "Everyone has a father," he said before he headed toward the office.

Sanjay understood David's point. Sure, most everyone had a father—and some of them were even harder to deal with than Mr. Patel. At least his father trusted him.

Sanjay's cell phone started to buzz. *Bstn 84, NY 91*, the text message read.

Sanjay cursed softly. He had money on that game. Fifty bucks down the toilet. Damn Celtics. He'd just managed to get the store accounts reconciled. Now he'd have to take out more cash.

He put the phone back in his pocket. This was a problem. A serious problem.

*Maybe Jerrica is my solution . . .*

***

The Joshua tree in Mike's front yard leaned toward the front curb as though it were reaching for visitors, trying to pull them into the tidy brown ranch house behind it. Some of the neighbors had tried to have the front yard declared an eyesore. Mike's mother was an avid gardener, and she had spent several years collecting native Nevada grasses and trees and planting them in the yard. That meant that there was no lawn, just sandy soil and spiky, dangerous-looking plants rimmed by white stones. Kat loved it, thought it was weird and beautiful.

When she pulled up, Mike was in the driveway, bent over his truck's engine. That truck—a vintage fifties Chevy—was his pride and joy. He'd picked it up cheap and overhauled the engine, then got a buddy to give it a custom paint job—cherry red with white trim. Every time Kat had sat next to him in that truck, she'd spent the entire ride wishing that someone would see *her*—the coolest girl on the planet. Some of the kids at her new school were rich. Some of them drove Audis; one guy even drove a Hummer. But anyone with money could drive those cars. Mike's vintage truck was unique. It meant he had skills. It meant he had style.

A red bandanna stuck out of the right rear pocket of Mike's faded jeans, and he was wearing a white tank stained with grease. It was only eleven o'clock on Sunday morning but already hot. A fine film of sweat made his skin gleam. Mike was like a fleck of iron pyrite—golden hair, golden eyes, golden skin—but he was no pretty boy. There was something about the cut of his nose and the sharp line of his jaw that made others uneasy and kept him from being what most people considered handsome.

Mike was humming along with the battered radio set on the ground beside the front tire as Kat walked up behind him.

"Hey," Kat said softly. She felt the word drop from her lips like juice from a peach.

For a moment, Mike was perfectly still. Then, slowly, he turned, pulling the bandanna from his pocket and wiping his hands. He squinted at her, as though he wasn't sure he remembered who she was.

Kat cleared her throat as Mike leaned against the truck's gleaming grille.

"How's it going?" Kat asked, trying again.

A frown and a nod told Kat that Mike was the same as usual. "Haven't seen you in a while." He shut the hood with a gentle clang.

Just then, the front door flew open. "Kat, is that you?" Mike's mother, Madeline, bustled onto the porch. She was holding a kitchen towel with a bright flower print on it, which she twisted in her hands. "How've you been, honey?"

Kat smiled at Madeline's chubby, beaming face. Her skin was pink and white, and a few strands of her gray-streaked blond hair had escaped from her casual ponytail. "I've been good," Kat replied.

"Ma, Kat's here to see me," Mike said.

Madeline ignored him. "How's school? How's Lala? Honey, are you eating enough? You look thin to me. Why don't you come inside and have a cookie and a chat with me once you're done talking to Mikey?"

"I can't stay long," Kat said, smiling a little at the sound of Mike's childhood nickname. Her eyes drifted to him, and she saw that he was watching the exchange between his mother and his ex-girlfriend with his arms folded across his chest.

"Well, honey, we sure do miss you around here." Madeline shot Mike a look. She'd always thought that Kat was a positive influence on her son. Kat suspected that Madeline would've loved to mother her.

"See you later, Ma," Mike told her.

"It's great seeing you again, Madeline," Kat said.

"You come and visit me anytime, Kat, do you hear me?" Mike and Madeline knew about Julia. Madeline flipped her kitchen towel over her shoulder and strode back inside. She closed the door a little harder than she needed to, in Kat's opinion.

When Kat turned back to face Mike, she caught his eyes skimming over her body. A hot flush ran up the back of her neck, and she suddenly wished that she had worn her denim skirt instead of jeans. Mike always liked seeing her in a skirt.

*Stop that,* Kat commanded herself. *You're here on business.*

His eyes met hers, and they were holding something. *A dare?* she wondered.

"So, Kitty Kat. What brings you by?"

The question sucked away all of her energy to lie, and she immediately forgot the story she'd concocted about being in the neighborhood and thinking about him and so on. Instead, she said, "I need an ID."

"Figured."

She watched him as he stepped away from the truck and laid a hand on the hood. Pursing his lips, he made a hmmm noise in an elaborate parody of someone mulling over something important.

"Come on, Mike, are you still doing that, or what?"

A shrug. "Why wouldn't I be?"

"So how much do you want?"

"How much do I want?" He leaned toward her so that his lips just brushed her ear. A shiver shuddered its way down Kat's neck as she realized that she could feel the heat from his body on her skin. "You know the answer to that."

Kat turned her face away from him, but she could still feel his breath on her neck. She felt her own breathing grow shallow—her throat was tight; she couldn't swallow. "You can't have that much."

"Just a little kiss." His voice was a whisper. "Just one. Is that such a huge deal?"

She didn't dare look into his eyes—she couldn't venture further than his lips. She knew their warmth, their softness. "It's a bad idea, Mike."

"Convince me."

Kat put a hand on his chest to push him away, but the touch drained her strength. She didn't push, didn't even resist as he leaned forward. The warm sweetness of his lips made her weak; made her cold, then hot. The kiss went on, and Kat felt her arm curl around his neck, her fingers twine through his long hair . . .

He pulled away suddenly, and when Kat opened her eyes, she saw the smirk at the corner of his mouth; he looked triumphant, and a bit pissed off. Quickly, Kat pulled her hand away from his neck. She touched her lips with her fingers—his taste was still on them.

"So," Mike said, suddenly all business, "who needs this ID—Sanjay?"

The mention of Kat's boyfriend's name sent a blush across her cheeks, and Mike smiled to see it. "Someone he knows," Kat admitted. She held out the small photo with a girl's face against a blue background.

Holding the photo carefully, Mike studied Jerrica's image. "Pretty," he said at last.

The word irked her, but Kat wasn't about to show it. "Will you do it?"

"Bring sixty bucks Wednesday night," Mike told her. "I'll have it here by eight-thirty."

"So no discount?" Kat asked as he headed into the garage.

Mike turned to face her, his white teeth flashing. "You should have paid *me* for that kiss," he said.

CHAPTER
SIX

**j**errica shifted on her stool and tapped the table for another card. With the precision of a pickpocket, the dealer slipped a card from the shoe and flipped it over. A seven. Left her with eighteen. She knew she'd probably lose this hand, but she didn't care. She was playing the minimum bet, five dollars a hand. So far, she was down less than a hundred dollars. The cards had been stone cold for the past half hour—she'd only taken the blackjack twice.

Jerrica had been in a casino before—who hadn't? In Vegas, everything was a casino. Even the pharmacy had slot machines that blinked and pinged while you bought your aspirin or Preparation H. Jerrica had even been to many of the big casinos on the Strip when her father was entertaining friends from out of town. Most of the best restaurants in town were in the casinos.

Still, walking into a casino was always a shock to the system. The smell of stale cigarette smoke and the flashing lights that blinked insanely across the wide patterned carpets, all competing for attention like manic children. The perfect twilight that made casino time stand still at five p.m. so that business travelers who arrived at three in the morning could have the same experience as the couple from Utah who arrived at seven p.m. The incessant mechanical dings and chirps of the slots paired with the silence of the zombie-like people staring at the machines, the dealers, the dice, the cards, while around them others chatted and snapped photos.

"Why don't we try a more low-key casino?" Jerrica had asked as Sanjay drove the Strip toward the toga-and-sandal-themed Vesuvius. "Start small."

"No, this is better." Sanjay steered straight ahead, negotiating the heavy traffic. Above them, the sky was dark, but neon lights made the Strip bright as day. "Nobody will notice us, not with all of the tourists they get in there. Friday nights are crazy. Trust me."

So far, their strategy was working. The dealer had asked to see Jerrica's ID, given a distracted glance at the driver's license that Mike had provided, and been satisfied. The casinos weren't supposed to let anyone who was under twenty-one place a bet. But the fact was, they didn't have much incentive to stop teens from gambling. It was an equal opportunity system, after all—everyone had the same chance to lose their money.

But Jerrica wouldn't lose.

The kaleidoscope numbers were starting to appear more regularly. Sometimes the geometric pattern was hazy and left her with a strange, hollow feeling of déjà vu. When that happened, Jerrica was never sure if the card would appear. But other times, the number flooded her mind with head-spinning vibrancy, shocking her out of the realm of reality and into another locale altogether—a place that was pure number. It was at those times that Jerrica could be sure that her card would be the next to turn up.

She still wasn't sure of the equations—she couldn't tell why one number and not another. Jerrica knew $x$ but didn't know how to find $y$. Not yet. But she was getting closer. It was all there, locked in her mind—she was sure of it. All she had to do was figure out how to get to it.

Jerrica had started with pi, the number that can be calculated to an infinite number of decimal places, never repeating, never showing a pattern. Pi is everywhere in nature, repeated endlessly in every circle, in every sphere. The DNA double helix revolves around pi. Pi appears in all sorts of waves and ripples—including color spectra and sound waves. Jerrica looked up at the nearby faux facade of the Parthenon that framed Sanjay's figure as he signaled for another card. Here was another mathematical marvel—the real Parthenon's architecture was based on the golden ratio: 1.618, or phi.

Actually, saying that phi was equal to 1.618 was like saying that pi was equal to 3.14. Phi could be calculated to thousands of decimal points. But what interested Jerrica was the fact that phi existed everywhere. It was another number that nature seemed to know and that humans seemed to have buried in their subconscious.

A couple of years ago, she had learned that phi could be derived through a sequence of numbers discovered by a man named Leonardo Pisano, known as Fibonacci. Fibonacci discovered that if a pair of rabbits produced another pair every month and each pair began breeding the second month, the process would be as follows: 0, 1, 1, 2, 3, 5, 8, 13, 21, and so on. Each successive number was the sum of the two before it. And if you divided any of the Fibonacci numbers after the number 2 by its preceding number, the answer approached 1.6. And as the numbers in the sequence grew, the result of their division came nearer and nearer to phi. The answers oscillated up or down, but they did not stop their march toward the golden ratio.

The ratio was everywhere—in the spiral of a nautilus shell, in the placement of a dorsal fin on a dolphin, in the exact proportions of a tiger's face. But what fascinated Jerrica was the human mind's *intuition* of phi. Why else would the Greeks have based the architecture of the Parthenon on the golden ratio?

And then there were clouds.

"Do you see those clouds?" she had asked Sanjay as they sat together in her kitchen that afternoon.

Through the window, at the edge of the sky, sat a diaphanous white curtain—a series of filmy strips across the wide blue void.

"Do you see how they're broken into ribbons?" she asked. "Does it remind you of anything?"

Sanjay shrugged. "Waves. Waves in a lake."

"Have you ever seen photographs of sand dunes?"

Sanjay paused for a moment, thinking. He reached for a pack of cigarettes in the pocket of his jacket, forgetting that he had kicked the habit months earlier. "Aren't they smooth?"

Jerrica shook her head. "The sand forms patterns across the top—ripples in the shape of the wind."

"So?"

"Clouds, dunes, waves—everything in the universe is just another expression of the same patterns, the same sequencing. The clouds, your DNA, a seashell—it's all math. Do you know Jackson Pollock?"

"The artist?" Sanjay's hand, having given up the search for cigarettes, rested on the table. "Drippy paintings?"

"Right. Do you know what a fractal is?"

"Jesus, I feel like I'm on *Jeopardy!* Which is the most annoying game show in the universe, by the way."

"Do you?"

"It's a shape. When you look at a smaller piece, it looks the same as the larger piece. When you look at a larger piece, it looks the same as a smaller chunk."

"Pollock's paintings are fractals." Jerrica felt a chill as she said the words. "He didn't do it intentionally. He made them intuitively. The fractals are an expression of his mind. Gaming is the same."

"And you're telling me this because . . ."

"Because that's what I think I'm doing. I'm intuiting the math in these games. I just can't quite quantify it. Not perfectly. I have the images, but not the equations."

"So—you're not psychic?"

"No."

"Are you saying," Sanjay said slowly, "that you think there's an equation that organizes the entire universe?" He watched as she scribbled something—he couldn't see what—in her notebook, the one with the marbleized cover. Would she ever trust him enough to show him what was on those pages?

"More like a *set* of principles," Jerrica corrected him. She could already see the numbers and letters in her mind. "A series of equations. I'm just—I'm just looking for the constant. I'm . . ." She shrugged, unwilling to admit that she was feeling her way through things.

Sanjay looked at her with a penetrating gaze. She quivered slightly, then forced herself to stay still. His brown eyes were narrowed, and Jerrica could tell that he was skeptical about her ideas. But that was okay. She was skeptical, too.

In a way, she found the skepticism comforting. It was thrilling to be on the verge of such an enormous mystery. Jerrica was just happy that she wasn't alone. This boy was with her.

\*\*\*

In the casino, Sanjay took another blackjack round and chatted easily with the overweight older woman in the seat beside him, telling her that he was an NYU student visiting Vegas with friends and that he was having the time of his life. He never made eye contact with Jerrica—just focused his attention on the woman, the dealer, and the cards. If Jerrica started winning, she could be spotted as an advantaged player. Once that happened, the casino could ask her to leave. That was why Sanjay did the actual betting. That way, if he was spotted, it wouldn't necessarily mean the end for both of them. Not that they were likely to be noticed—their bets were too low. Not only that, the way they bet—never doubling down or splitting their cards—added to the impression of unsophisticated amateurs.

Jerrica tuned out most of Sanjay's chatter, along with the rattles and pings of the slot machines behind her. Her mind drifted as she watched a woman dressed as a Vegas-inspired Grecian walk by. She was so distracted that she almost didn't notice that she had made blackjack.

"Hey, look at that!" Sanjay said.

A king and an ace sat on the table in front of her. Her head felt light, and warmth sank into her as if she were a sponge dipped in bathwater—she was surprised at how powerful she felt at having taken a hand. Not that it was a huge amount of money—after all, she'd been betting the minimum. But she had won.

"Congratulations," the dealer, a moonfaced man, said as he handed her some chips.

"Thank you," Jerrica whispered.

She and Sanjay played awhile longer. Every now and again, Jerrica would give Sanjay a signal to bet (hand on the wooden edge of the table in front of her) or to stay (hand in her lap). Slowly and steadily, they won. Together, they were up by four hundred, then eight hundred, then thirteen hundred. "All right, that's all for me," Sanjay said at last. "Quit while I'm ahead—something I never do." He winked at the dealer and traded in his chips for black ones, then walked toward the cage to cash them in.

The dealer didn't see him slip a black chip into the back pocket of Jerrica's black pants. Nobody saw it. Jerrica barely even felt it, but she knew it was there. Sanjay didn't want to cash out more than three thousand dollars at a time—that was the limit. Any more than that and they wanted you to fill out a cash transaction report. They were way under that now, which was a good thing.

Jerrica played another two losing hands, then slid off her stool, announcing, "I think I'm done."

The other players didn't look up as she walked away.

Burns a hole in your pocket—that's what they say about money. Well, Jerrica could feel that black chip searing into her flesh. Hooking a long finger into the pocket, she fished out the chip. It was warm from her skin. One black chip. One hundred dollars.

Around her, the noise whirred and pinged, the lights flashed. At one side of the casino floor was a line of tables, each with a black rectangular sign showing a series of red numbers: the last seven numbers to come up on the roulette wheel.

Jerrica didn't altogether feel her body moving as she walked toward the tables. It was more like she was floating—or as if her body had broken down and dissolved, then reappeared at the table.

Seven. Double zero. Thirty. Fourteen. Twenty-three. Ten. Nineteen.

Jerrica knew that Sanjay was waiting for her. She was supposed to cash out and meet him by the cage. The black-and-red wheel spun, and the ball bounced and skipped across the pockets at the bottom, falling neatly into its destined place. Across her eyes, colors flashed. Blue, green, pink, yellow. The colors swirled—forming a starburst, a pinwheel, a vortex—and she felt herself plummet, like Alice down the rabbit hole, spinning, flailing, plummeting. The dealer called for bets and Jerrica felt herself falling, falling—moving through space like a tiny pinprick of light, like a shooting star, like a meteor. And without knowing her own movements, she stepped forward and placed her black chip on thirty-three.

The wheel slowed. The white marble danced, landing once on eight, then popping out again, and finally whirling around and around, secure in its bed. Thirty-three.

Thirty-three. Jerrica blinked. Then again. And suddenly the casino snapped back into place around her and she knew where she was.

The others at the table—Jerrica hadn't even realized there were others at the table—gasped when they realized what had just happened. The dealer paid off the players, then shoved thirty-five black chips toward Jerrica. She collected them and staggered off, numb.

"Hey," Sanjay said, catching her by the elbow near the cage. "Hey, are you okay?"

"I think I need some air," Jerrica told him.

Sanjay nodded, steering her expertly through the crowds and out into the warm night air. He didn't stop until they reached his car, where he opened the door for her and waited while she got settled.

"Did you cash out?" Sanjay asked as he opened his door and slid into the seat.

"No." Jerrica stared straight ahead.

"What?"

She turned to him and held up her purse. Then she stuck her hand inside and pulled out a fistful of black chips.

"Holy shit!" Sanjay backed against the car door as if the chips were snakes. "What did you do?"

Jerrica laughed to see his eyes so wide. He actually looked frightened. "I won," she told him.

"Roulette?" The word twisted over Sanjay's tongue like a roller coaster. "You can't win at roulette. It's just chance."

Jerrica dropped the chips into her bag and sat back in her seat. "I know," she said.

"Holy crap. Holy, holy. Crap." Sanjay's mind was spinning like rubber tires against cement, practically squealing, leaving skid marks. He grabbed the bag. "What did you do? You put it on one number? Thirty-five to one—you've got thirty-five hundred dollars in here?"

"Yeah."

"Okay. Okay." Sanjay took a deep breath, raking his long fingers through his hair. "We'll have to cash them in over a couple of days, that's all. No big deal."

"I want you to take it."

"What?"

"The money."

"Why?"

"I don't want it." Jerrica's voice was firm.

Sanjay held up his hands in surrender. "I can't—"

"I don't want to deal with the money, Sanjay, okay?" She thought about the chip that had nearly burned a hole in her pocket. The one that had caused her to win this embarrassing heap. Everyone at the table had turned to look at her—it had made her uncomfortable. "I just want to study the math. The money part—it's too much pressure."

"I don't think—"

"I don't *want* it, Sanjay."

They sat in the car for a very long time, staring out at the darkness of the parking garage. Jerrica felt like a fish in a fishbowl. It was some version of safe—as long as she didn't try to step outside, she could breathe. She felt warmth radiating from Sanjay's side of the car and a wave of gratitude for his presence. He understood her. Besides, she could read the hunger in his eyes. He wanted that money. And she could give it to him. Pleasure sprouted in her, like a seedling, at this small power.

"Okay," Sanjay said at last, amazed at how all of his problems had been solved, just like that. One breath and the world was one way. Another breath and everything had changed.

He turned the key in the ignition, and they were off.

***

"Jerrica, come eat with us," her father said from the doorway that linked the kitchen to the dining room. Jerrica was sitting in the breakfast nook, crisply turning over card after card. The queen hit the table with a gentle snap. She knew what that meant. The queen was her; she was the queen. She scribbled a line in the small spiral notebook beside her right hand.

"In a minute." Jerrica's reply was automatic.

Mr. Tyler leaned against the clean white doorframe, watching his daughter with an amused half smile on his face. "What are you doing?"

"Playing cards."

Her father watched for another moment before saying, "What game is that?"

Irritation stabbed into her chest like a grappling hook, tugging at her innards. Couldn't he see that she was busy? "It's not a game."

Jerrica laid another card into place beside the queen. A ten of diamonds. She looked that up in the book beside her. Ten of pentacles: fortuitous change, imminent good fortune. She scrawled in the notebook.

The hairs at the top of her head started to prickle, and she realized that her father was still watching her. She looked up into those familiar green eyes, the same as her own, and couldn't help wondering if the baby (her brother? her sister?) would have their green eyes. Angela's were brown. Those genes were dominant, weren't they? For some reason, she didn't want the baby to have green eyes.

Jerrica stared back silently. She waited, counting slowly to twenty, but he didn't walk out. Instead, he stepped toward the kitchen table. He laid a hand on the book and spun it to face him. "*Browning's Introduction to the Tarot?*" he asked, reading the title.

The grappling hook tugged harder. "That's right."

"You're reading fortunes?"

Jerrica took a breath, held it, released it. "Modern cards are based on the tarot deck," she explained.

Mr. Tyler shook his head. "So?" He slipped his hands into the front pockets of his jeans. Jerrica's dad was the kind of guy who changed out of his office clothes the moment he got home. *Like Mister Rogers,* Jerrica thought. Right now, he was even wearing a green cardigan.

"So . . ." She paused, tempted to tell him what she was doing— that she was searching the cards for patterns, for meaning. She wanted to tell him that the cards were trying to tell her something. That they were whispering meanings all the time—showing her patterns that became numbers that became outcomes. "It's for a history project," Jerrica said at last. This was her latest discovery: some lies are better than the truth.

Mr. Tyler nodded. If there was one thing he respected, it was schoolwork.

"Andy, what's taking so long?" Angela asked, appearing in the doorway. A frown line linking the edge of her nose to the corner of her mouth stood out like a scar. "Are you two coming to the table or what?"

"I'm not hungry," Jerrica said, turning back to her cards.

"It's dinnertime," Angela snapped.

"Jerrica's working on a school project," Mr. Tyler said.

"I promise I'll eat something later," Jerrica said, turning over a four of spades. Spades—that was swords. Good news tempered with danger.

"Later it'll be cold, Jerrica," Angela said. "It's important for us to eat together as a fam—"

"Angie . . ." Mr. Tyler put a gentle hand on Angela's shoulder. "It's okay."

Angela made a clicking sound with her tongue that told Jerrica that it wasn't okay. But she wasn't the mother. She wasn't even the stepmother—not yet. In the end, she couldn't do much more than to put her palms in the air and say "Fine," which is what she did.

"It would make Angela really happy if you would join us for a while," Mr. Tyler said.

"I will," Jerrica lied. "In a few minutes."

Finally he left.

Jerrica flipped over another card. A six of diamonds. Diamonds were good—they meant money, at least according to *Browning's*. It wasn't that Jerrica believed that the cards could foretell the future, not exactly. But she couldn't help wondering if there might be more to her predictions than just knowing what card would come up next. After all, the gift had to mean something, didn't it? What was the point of being able to predict cards if you couldn't also predict other—more useful—things? *I'm not just a monkey with a trick.*

She scribbled in her notebook and turned over a new card.

"She barely eats." Angela's voice drifted in from the dining room. Jerrica could never figure out whether Angela couldn't tell how easy it was to overhear things in the echoey house or if she actually wanted Jerrica to hear her opinions. Jerrica secretly thought that it was Angela's passive-aggressive way of letting her future stepdaughter know that she didn't approve of her.

"She's a teenager; what do you expect?" Mr. Tyler replied. "They're always on some diet or another."

"All she does is sit in her room and play cards," Angela said. "It isn't normal."

"You were the one who said that we needed to give her some room," Jerrica's father said. "I thought we were giving her time."

Jerrica's hand paused over the next card. She could hear the clink of Angela's fork against the white china plate. Angela was very into proper meals, served with a protein, a vegetable, a starch, and a linen napkin. Before she came into their lives, it had been spaghetti and microwave Thai noodles, still Jerrica's favorite foods. She missed those noodles.

"Fine," Angela said at last.

Jerrica turned over the next card. Five of hearts. Hearts were cups. A good omen.

Jerrica thought about the thirty-three—the roulette number. She knew that if she asked the professor, he would point out that her odds of winning were one in thirty-eight. She might, after all, have just gotten lucky.

Whatever that meant.

Jerrica thought about the certainty—the colors she had seen

before she put down the chip. It was the strongest vision she'd ever had—almost as if she had received a message. Carl Jung had once written about the reservoir of human experience. Perhaps the math was located there—already in her brain. Was it so impossible? In a world governed by the golden ratio, in a universe that recognized pi in countless places, couldn't the Principles already exist, untapped? And couldn't they apply to everything?

And here was the ultimate question:

If she could predict outcomes . . . couldn't she change them?

Jerrica turned over another card. Jack of hearts. The rakish grin on the jack's face reminded her of Sanjay, and she felt her blood quicken in her veins.

She made another mark in her notebook.

"Kat," Trish said in a low voice. She ran her finger around the edge of her mug, slowing down at the chipped place near the handle. There was a similar chip at the very tip of her hot-pink nail polish, and Kat marveled at the symmetry. "We need to talk. Richard Nelson called today."

Kat sat very still. The sun leaked in through the small, grimy windows over the kitchen sink. "What did he want?"

"He wanted to discuss your mother's parole hearing."

"Oh." Kat nodded. She'd buried the letter at the bottom of her underwear drawer, but she couldn't stop what was already in motion.

"He said she has a good chance of getting out . . ." Trish's right shoulder twitched into a half shrug. "He thinks it might be helpful if you were to say something on her behalf. Remind everyone that it was an accident. That you were hysterical, and she didn't know what to do . . ." Trish picked up her coffee, grimacing as she took a sip.

"I told them everything already." Kat rested her elbow against the table and cupped her hand over her mouth and chin. Of course, she hadn't told them *everything.*

"But this is a parole hearing. They're going to determine who gets custody—"

A chill ran up Kat's arms. Custody. In a flash, she saw her mother the way she had looked that night. When she got home, her hair was disheveled and her expression wild, her eyes unfocused. It was late—well past midnight—but Julia didn't ask why Kat was still awake, sitting on the ugly orange chair and watching TV.

Julia was moving quickly, but not with the eager, jumpy joy of those nights that she came home a winner. If she had won, she would have been a contained mass of frantic energy, like a shaken bottle of soda. Once, when Julia had won big, she woke up Lala and Kat and made them get dressed in the middle of the night. Kat remembered pulling on her pink Keds and helping her sister yank on a flowered dress and green leggings while it was still dark. They had gone to a twenty-four-hour Wal-Mart, where their mother had handed them each a hundred dollars and told them to get whatever they wanted. Kat could still hear the squeak of Lala's rubber sandals as she bolted toward the toys . . .

But there were no midnight trips that night.

Instead, Julia had rushed to the kitchen for another drink.

"She might be home in a matter of weeks," Trish said, breaking up Kat's thoughts. Images dissolved in the air around her. Trish's eyes were searching. She didn't know everything about Kat's life with Julia. But sometimes Kat got the sense that Trish suspected more than she let on.

"And then we'd go back to her?" Kat asked.

Trish ran her fingers through her hair with both hands, pulling it tight, away from her face. "I guess you'd have to."

Kat placed her hands on either side of her black plate. The smooth surface was smeared with yellow egg, the remnants of her breakfast, and suddenly she felt ill. "All right," Kat said at last.

Trish gave Kat's hand a sympathetic pat.

Kat wanted to ask, *Couldn't we stay with you?* But she hated to beg. If her aunt wanted her nieces to stay, it was up to her to say something.

Outside, the sun passed behind a cloud, turning the dingy kitchen momentarily dim. The low light lingered, then suddenly brightened as the sun came out again.

*What are you going to do about it?*

Sanjay's words echoed in her mind. Yes. She had to *do* something. That much was clear.

But what?

If she told the truth, wouldn't she be an accessory to the crime? At the very least she'd lied under oath. That was definitely a crime. What if they put her in juvie? Even if it was only for a few months, who would take care of Lala?

Every time Kat thought of the secret her mother had forced on her, Kat's stomach clenched and thin fog poured into her mind. She took in a sharp breath, forcing herself back into the moment. *What you need,* she told herself, *is some kind of plan. So think. Think!*

Trish didn't say anything else, and Kat just carried her plate to the sink, acid blood burning through her veins.

CHAPTER
EIGHT

*the trick is trying not to think.* The calculations were already finished in her too-fast-for-thought mind, and second-guessing could do her in. So she didn't think. Instead, she focused on feeling her pulse in her ears. She could do that if she was very still. Jerrica felt her blood pulsing, and paid particular attention to her breath. If she was relaxed—relaxed and patient—the kaleidoscope appeared and the betting came as second nature. It wasn't perfectly consistent—the patterns didn't always show up—but they came often enough to keep Sanjay and her ahead.

Here is how Jerrica signaled Sanjay where to bet: Jerrica always put down five chips. One on a decoy number; then two on either a split or a corner. As she picked up her hand, she drew her thumb across the next number that she expected would come up. Sanjay would place two chips on a different split or corner of the same number. Then he would place one or two other bets down, it didn't matter where.

They kept the bets small, but they won consistently. The casinos considered roulette unbeatable. They didn't watch the players the way they watched players at the blackjack tables. Unless they suspected the croupier, the security eyes that watched from behind cameras placed all over the casino had no reason to think that anyone could control winnings at the wheel.

*The myth of random chance.*

"Place your bets," the croupier said. She had short black hair and a crisp, efficient manner that Jerrica liked.

The room spun slightly and a gleaming violet reflection leaped into Jerrica's eye from the rim of the wheel. Instantly, she plunged into a vortex of colors and shapes, a swirling eddy of green and purple . . . Jerrica placed her chip on six. Then one across the line between twenty-two and twenty-one. She drew her fingers lightly across the twenty-two as she placed two chips on the corner of a thirteen.

Sanjay put a chip down on the twenty-one corner, then tossed a chip at double zero and one on black.

"I'm doing what you do." A bald man in a short-sleeved button-down placed a chip on double zero and winked at Sanjay. "Seems like you've been on a streak."

"I sure have," Sanjay said with a wide smile. He patted his pile of chips playfully, as if it was a pet. "Lady Luck seems to like me tonight."

"I still can't believe I'm here in Las Vegas." Colorful neon lights were reflected on the top of the man's pink scalp. "I've always dreamed of coming here."

"I know what you mean," Sanjay said warmly. "My friends back in Philly are totally jealous."

"You're from Philly?" The bald man beamed. His bland face reminded Jerrica of a toy she used to have—Weebles, they were called. They were advertised as a toy that wobbled but could never fall down. Of course, the advertisers had never counted on a child like Jerrica, who had smashed her Weeble into the thick pink pile carpeting in her bedroom to keep it on its side. She had wanted to make a point.

There was something about this Weeble that bothered her. She felt as if she had seen him before—as if he kept popping up, like the toy. *He has one of those faces,* she thought. *The kind that always looks familiar, but you can never quite place.* Casinos were full of guys just like this—bald and badly dressed—and it was starting to unnerve her.

"My wife's from Philly," Weeble said to Sanjay. "And my son's in school there."

Sanjay hedged: "Uh, I'm from outside the city." He hadn't meant to draw the man into conversation. He just enjoyed pretending to be someone else at these tables. Sanjay liked to think about the person on his fake ID—who he was, where he came from—and try to become that person.

"Where? Media?" Weeble asked as the croupier gave the last call for bets. The white ball skimmed the wheel's rim, moving in perfect counterpoint to the numbered checkerboard flashes. The dark-haired woman's eyes flowed to Sanjay's face, then flicked to Jerrica's. She held Jerrica's eyes a beat too long, then turned back to the wheel.

*She realizes we're together,* Jerrica thought. From beneath her false lashes and blue eyeshadow, the croupier saw right through them. This was bad. She knew that Jerrica was signaling Sanjay from across the table. Once the casinos realized that you had an edge, they had every right to ask you to leave.

"No, it's a little suburb—you've never heard of it." Sanjay leaned against the table, not even watching the wheel as it slowed. The white ball jumped and skipped, dancing across the slots.

The man pushed: "Try me."

Jerrica glared at Sanjay. He wasn't looking at her, but she was certain that he could feel the heat from her stare. It was hot enough to melt flesh. He had walked right into this. She knew that he didn't know the first thing about Pennsylvania. She touched her lips—their signal that something was wrong—but Sanjay didn't look up. He was ignoring her.

"Eastonia?" Sanjay said.

Weeble thought for a minute. "Can't say I've ever heard of it. What's it near?"

*Please don't say Latvia,* Jerrica begged silently.

"It's not too far from Media." Sanjay ran a hand through his thick hair. Jerrica had seen him make that gesture before, always when he was uncomfortable.

"It's funny, because I thought I knew every place around Philly." Weeble sipped his drink. "Susan—that's my wife—her relatives live in five different suburbs. I'll have to check a map the next time we go."

The croupier cast another look in Sanjay's direction, but in the next moment the ball settled. "The number is twenty-two," she said. "Twenty-two is the winner."

"You won again!" Weeble announced, clapping Sanjay on the back as the croupier handed out chips with her usual efficiency. "You've got the eye, I'm telling you! This time, I'm putting all my chips down on top of yours!"

Sanjay laughed and looked up at Jerrica as he pulled his chips across the felt. She felt her face burn. The croupier called for bets, and Sanjay winked.

Jerrica tipped the croupier a fifty and walked away from the table. "I'd like to cash out," she told the thick man behind the cage. She passed him her ID and nine hundred dollars in chips, keeping five hundred in her bag. Two hours of slow, steady tortoise winnings. Exactly according to plan.

He took the chips and counted out the money in crisp fifties. Then he placed the bills in an envelope and handed it to Jerrica, who shoved it into her bag.

"What are you doing?"

Jerrica jumped. Sanjay was leaning against the wall beside her, arms folded across his chest. "I'm leaving," Jerrica told him, recovering.

"Why?"

Jerrica stalked toward the exit. "People aren't supposed to know we're together. That was the whole idea, Sanjay—you're supposed to be the primary bettor." It wasn't her idea; Sanjay had gotten the idea from a book he'd read. Jerrica hadn't really seen the point, but she went along with it. "I'm just working out the Principles."

"Nobody's watching roulette," Sanjay said, matching her pace.

"That croupier was watching you."

"So what?"

"She knew you were lying."

"They can't prove shit," Sanjay insisted.

Jerrica didn't break her stride. She was three steps from the door when Sanjay grabbed her hand. "Jerrica," he said.

"What?"

She was looking at the ground, and Sanjay inclined his head below hers and smiled up into her face. "You're not mad at me, are you?"

A shiver ran across her shoulders, tickling her like a feather. "Yes. I am."

"You're mad? Really?" Sanjay blinked, then pouted. "Because the croupier was looking at me?"

"She was suspicious, Sanjay," Jerrica said. "So was that bald guy. We have to be careful, all right?"

"Okay," he said. "I'm sorry."

"Good. Now let go of my hand."

"No." He curled his warm fingers through hers.

Jerrica sighed, and her black bangs fluttered. "You're annoying me," she said, although the gentle pressure of his fingertips shot a thrill through her.

"How can I be annoying when I'm so cute?" Sanjay demanded. "Look, I'm holding your hand. And now I'm going to take you out to dinner . . ." He smiled, showing the deep dimple in his right cheek. "Let's hit a buffet!" Sanjay tucked her hand against his waist, as if she were a handbag.

She resisted the pleasure she felt at being treated like one of his possessions.

Jerrica huffed a quiet laugh as she stumbled after him. It was too hard to resist Sanjay. And he knew it.

As they swooped through the revolving door and stepped out into the warm air, Jerrica cast one last look behind her, into the casino. "Sanjay," she said.

"What?" He kept walking.

"Nothing," Jerrica said. For a moment, she was sure that she had caught sight of Weeble's face—that from his place across the casino he was watching them. But now he was gone.

*Maybe I imagined it,* Jerrica thought.

*Maybe.*

***

"What are you doing?"

"Ow, dammit!" Kat rubbed her head where she had smashed it against the doorframe. "It's not funny," Kat said, even though she really didn't blame her sister for giggling. She knew she must look ridiculous—crawling around the bottom of her closet, butt out, and jumping at the slightest noise. "Don't you know how to knock?" Kat grabbed a boot and shoved a small wad of bills inside.

"Is that money?" Lala asked.

Kat slid the boot back into place in the darkest corner of her already dark closet. "If you touch it, the cops will never find your body."

"I wouldn't take your money." Lala looked offended.

Kat stood up, dusting off her hands, which were filthy, thanks to that boot. It was half of a pair she hadn't worn since eighth grade. Kat knew she should throw them away, but the thought made her anxious. "I know," she admitted . . . grudgingly. Lala was "pathologically honest," in Trish's words. She didn't lie, didn't steal—wouldn't even cheat at Monopoly. She was good. Really, really good. The thing that amazed Kat was how effortless Lala's goodness was. She didn't even have to think about it.

Lala flung herself dramatically across Kat's bed, her long, dark hair spilling over the edge. "What's it for?" she asked the ceiling.

"What?"

Lala rolled over onto her side and watched as Kat sat on the edge of the bed. Automatically, Lala slid over to give her sister more room. "The money," she said.

"For a rainy day."

"No, really—what for?"

Kat looked her dead in the eye. "It's for *rain,* Lala," she said. It had only recently occurred to Kat that money might just be the answer to her problems. If she could save up enough, maybe she could take off before the parole hearing even appeared on the calendar. But she only had about seventy dollars. Enough to take her and Lala exactly nowhere.

"Jeez, sorry I asked," Lala said, flopping backward again.

Kat heard a door slam. Trish was home.

"Kat . . . ," Lala said slowly, as if she had been thinking something over. She turned her face to look at her sister so that her cheek was pressed against the scratchy olive blanket that covered Kat's bed.

"Yes?" Kat arched an eyebrow at her.

Lala winced, scrunching up her face, then peeked out of one eye. "Can I have twenty-three dollars?"

Kat snorted. "That didn't take long."

"I need it," Lala said.

"Well, then, by all means, help yourself." Kat gestured grandly to the closet. "Feel free to take fistfuls of the money I've been saving and just—"

"Forget it, forget it—"

"—just go to the mall and get yourself a makeover, or maybe a new pair of socks, or—oh, I know!—how about a *scented candle?*"

"I said, forget it." Sighing in frustration, Lala slapped her hand against Kat's mattress. It bounced back slightly, and something about the futility of that gesture made Kat clamp her mouth shut.

Grudging silence settled over the room. Kat felt like a resentful hen perched on her eggs, fluffed out and indignant at the presence of a passing cat. But a moment later, once the cat went by, she found herself wondering why it had wandered into the coop in the first place.

"Why?" Kat asked finally.

"You don't care," Lala said flatly, "so why are you even asking?"

"I care," Kat said. She hoped it didn't sound as lame as she thought it did.

Lala's eyebrows crept up, and she looked at her sister as if she was studying her. She opened her mouth as if she was about to spill, then seemed to decide against it. "No—forget it. You'll think it's stupid."

"I won't," Kat told her.

"You will, because it *is* stupid," Lala said.

"Tell me anyway."

Lala groaned a little. "The photos are back."

"What photos?"

"Picture day."

"And—what? You look hideous? Everyone looks hideous in those—"

"No, no—" Lala sat up and folded her legs Indian-style. Her tiny pink socks were tucked under her knees. "Look, lots of people have promised me their photo. But Trish says that those pictures are a rip-off. And if I can't give people my photo—"

"They won't give you theirs." Kat nodded, remembering. Those pictures were like trading cards—collect all your best friends. The idea was to get a brick of them to lug around in your bag so you could prove how much everyone liked you.

And everyone liked Lala.

"That *is* stupid," Kat agreed.

Lala closed her eyes and shook her head. "I know. You're right."

Kat pressed her lips together. "I'll give you the money," she said after a moment.

"You will?" Lala's dark eyes popped open.

*She looks like I've just told her that she's won the lottery,* Kat thought. Lala was so happy.

*Isn't it bad enough that we have to live with our aunt?* Kat thought bitterly. *That neither one of us knows our dads? That our mom is in prison?*

Kat went to the closet and pulled some money out of her boot. "Take it," she said, handing it over. "And don't tell Trish."

"Why not?" Lala asked.

Kat blew out a frustrated breath. "I just don't want her to know, okay? She may get mad if she finds out that you came to me for money." It was the kind of thing that Julia would have flipped out about. Even though they had been living with Trish for over a year, Kat still didn't feel like she completely understood her aunt. She mostly dealt with her by avoiding her.

Lala was standing now, staring at the money like it fell out of the sky. "I won't say anything," she promised, folding the bills. She flung her arms around her sister's neck so suddenly that Kat almost fell over. "Thank you," she whispered. "Thankyouthankyouthankyou."

Kat patted her sister's hair awkwardly. "It's okay."

"What's going on in here?" Trish appeared at the doorway, her blue eyes tired. Trish wasn't as beautiful as Kat's mother, not by a long shot, but she had Julia's glossy blond hair and her strange laser gaze. Her look went to a primal place in Kat, and Kat froze. "Anybody getting hungry? Isn't it almost dinnertime?"

"Just about," Kat said.

Her aunt smiled at her. Kat didn't know Trish well, but she respected her. After all, their own grandparents had refused to take them in. When Julia was arrested, Trish had immediately come forward to take care of Kat and Lala. She was the only family member at the trial. Julia had never been close with her, but Trish was there when it mattered . . . in spite of the fact that she barely had two nickels to scrape together. Kat was grateful to her. Kat didn't even mind working part-time at the shoe store for minimum wage. She liked the fact that she could afford to buy new clothes sometimes or pay for Lala's pictures now. The money gave Kat a small sense of security.

"I just have to go to the bathroom," Lala said quickly. "I'll be right there."

"You're on table-setting," Trish told Lala as she headed toward the kitchen.

Before she hurried out the door, Lala cast another grateful look at Kat.

Kat felt her heart growing, expanding against her rib cage, threatening to burst out of her chest. *People always say money can't buy happiness,* she thought. *It only cost me twenty-three bucks.*

CHAPTER
NINE

j errica placed her bet on the line above the five and traced her
fingers lightly over the two that hovered over it. Then she placed
a decoy bet somewhere in the twenties, where Sanjay had just
unloaded two fifty-dollar chips. He picked up five black chips and
weighed them in his hand, scanning the roulette table as if decid-
ing where to place them.

Jerrica felt her chest tighten. *What the hell does he think he's doing?*
They were supposed to be keeping a low profile, slow and steady,
as Jerrica felt her way through the shifting kaleidoscope in her
mind. Sometimes the colors and shapes were hazy, sometimes
razor-sharp. They didn't win all the time. But usually—when the
image was as clear as it was at that moment—the right number
turned up. Now, if he put that on the corner bet, it would pay off
at eight to one—four thousand dollars—and that would definitely
catch someone's attention.

As if he could hear her thoughts, Sanjay looked up at Jerrica.
With a grin, he placed the stack cleanly in the center of the number two.

Jerrica's fingernails bit into her palm. Straight up, the payoff was thirty-five to one. *Dammit, Sanjay. Goddamn you.*

*I should've known.* He had been bitching the night before that they were taking too long, playing too cautiously. It was as if he had forgotten that it had to be like that. For one thing, the number kaleidoscopes didn't appear every time she played. True, they appeared more often and more vividly in the casinos than they did when she played cards by herself or online. But they weren't constant. Not yet.

He had been calling from a cell phone, but because of poor reception, the first few words of his complaint dropped out. ". . . doesn't even feel like gambling."

"If you want to make it more exciting, you can go by yourself," Jerrica had told him, casting a glance at her notebook. The pages were worn and crumpled between two heavily bruised covers. The notebook was almost full.

For a moment, Sanjay had been tempted to say that he *would* go by himself. The truth was, he had been doing plenty of betting without Jerrica. Horses, online poker, sports. It was just . . . with her, roulette had become like a job, and now he couldn't afford not to go on without her. Not now, when his credit cards were finally paid off; when the money from the store was finally back, tucked snugly into his father's bank account. "No, it's fine," Sanjay had said. "I'll see you tomorrow."

"Tomorrow." Jerrica had pressed the off button and put the receiver into its cradle on her bureau. Looking up, she caught sight of her reflection in the mirror. Her skin was pale, and dark circles bloomed beneath her green eyes. *I don't feel tired.* The Principles had kept her awake for the past three nights. Whenever she shut her eyes, she felt electricity pumping through her body. There was so much work to do—so many equations, so many proofs to work through. She didn't want to fall asleep and miss a clue.

Now she leaned against the roulette table for support as the croupier spun the wheel. She was hot. She needed to sit down.

*This is it,* Jerrica thought, watching a tiny smile play on Sanjay's lips as his black eyes flickered with the spinning wheel. *We're done for the night. If Sanjay wants to mess everything up, he can do it himself.*

A gasp hissed up from the table a moment before the croupier announced, "The winning number is two. Two is the winner!" A couple of young Australian guys started to applaud, and the rest of the table joined in. Sanjay smiled and gave a slight bow as the croupier paid off his chips.

Jerrica turned away, seething.

"Excuse me, sir?"

A tall, slim man with a scar that sliced a delicate *C* below the dark skin of his right eye was standing beside Sanjay.

"Excuse me, sir?" C nodded politely to Sanjay. "May I see your identification?"

Sanjay just kept on pouring chips into his pockets.

C tapped Sanjay on the shoulder. "Sir."

"Sure," Sanjay said smoothly. He pulled out his wallet and handed over his ID.

C looked at it closely, then looked at Sanjay. "I'd like to talk to you for a few moments, if you don't mind."

"I mind."

Jerrica couldn't believe that Sanjay could stay so cool. She felt as if someone had set her feet on fire. *What does he know? Does he suspect that Sanjay is underage—that his ID is a fake? Or has he spotted him as an advantaged player?*

Jerrica had heard rumors about what happened to people who

were spotted as advantaged players. They were banned from the casino where they were spotted and all the other ones linked to its security system. But there were wilder stories. Jerrica didn't know if these tales of people who managed to beat the system and then disappeared were true or not . . .

She wanted to run, escape, hide—but she stayed rooted to the spot in which she was standing.

"I'd like to have a word." C touched Sanjay's shoulder and Sanjay shook him off, hard.

"Get your hands off me," Sanjay snarled.

One of the Australians took a step forward—whether to defend Sanjay or help the security guard Jerrica wasn't sure. She felt a scream building up in her throat.

"Please come with me." C's voice was patient. He had all night, and he wasn't going to let up.

But Sanjay muscled past him, striding toward the exit.

C took off after him, but Sanjay was moving quickly. Security wouldn't lay a hand on him, not on the floor of the casino. Right?

The croupier called for bets.

"What the bloody hell was that?" one of the Australians—the one who had stepped forward—asked no one in particular.

Jerrica didn't stay to hear the answer.

***

"Hey, Kat." Bo Cravens squinted up at her, smiling through his mane of shaggy blond hair. "What's up?"

"Just waiting for Sanjay," Kat said as Bo walked up the steps and took a seat beside her. She tucked the novel she had been reading back into her bag. They were in front of the public library, which was a ten-minute walk from school and a half hour from her house. Bo, of course, didn't have to worry about walking anywhere. His father had bought him a car at the beginning of junior year, the nanosecond he turned sixteen.

"Sanjay?" Bo yanked his fingers through the long bangs that sat heavy over his eyes. The vague scent of patchouli—Kat could never decide if she loved it or loathed it—drifted up from his clothes. "Didn't I see him leaving the parking lot with that girl?"

"What girl?"

"That black-haired girl? You know her, man—Jessica." Bo tilted his face toward the fading sun.

"Jerrica?"

Bo thought for a moment. "Right. Jerrica."

Kat sighed. That figured. She had been sitting outside the library for the past thirty minutes, watching them tick by slowly as she waited for Sanjay to arrive. She'd called him on his cell phone twice, but the voice mail answered. Kat didn't bother leaving a message. What was the point? He could see that she had called. If he wanted to get in touch with her, he would.

Still, she thought it was a little strange that he didn't reply—usually Sanjay was glued to his cell.

"Well, I guess that explains things," Kat said at last.

Bo tugged at his navy T-shirt. His eyelids fluttered slightly, and he looked like he wished he hadn't said anything. "Sorry."

Kat felt the heat rise to her face, and she stood up to hide the blush. She hated it when people felt sorry for her. "No problem. I'm glad you told me. You know Sanjay—he never gets anywhere on time."

"Yeah." Bo jerked his head toward the door. "You want to come inside?"

"I should be getting home."

"I could give you a ride."

But Kat had already started down the steps. "I'm good," she said, giving him a slight wave. She didn't know if Bo was hitting on her or not, but she knew she wasn't interested. He wasn't her type at all.

Still, Kat found it disturbing how eager others seemed to be to report to her that Sanjay had been spotted in several different places with Jerrica. *Why aren't I mad or jealous or something?*

A truck honked behind Kat, making her jump. "Jesus, Mike," she said as he rolled down the glass. "What the hell?"

"Get in." He just leaned over and pushed open the door. She climbed into the seat, remembering what it was like to view the world from behind Mike's dashboard. She was surprised to discover that she still loved the chrome-rimmed vintage speedometer, the ancient AM-only radio.

Mike cast a glance in the rearview mirror, then pulled away from the curb.

"It's not a good idea to drive up behind a woman walking alone," Kat told him. "You scared the shit out of me."

"Sorry."

He drove three blocks, then pulled into the lot of a boarded-up Mobil station.

He turned the key in the ignition, and the truck coughed into silence. Mike turned to face her. His eyes held hers for a moment, and she sat back against her seat. "What?"

"Listen, I need you to do me a favor." His voice was low, and there wasn't a trace of his usual Mike smirk. His seriousness settled into the truck like another passenger.

"Tell me."

Mike reached beneath his seat and pulled out an ancient cigar box. He handed it to Kat. "Don't open it."

Her fingers hesitated over the box. "What is it?"

"You don't want to know." His golden gaze made her slightly breathless.

"Tell me." Her voice was a whisper.

He didn't answer, and she knew what that meant. *So he is dealing.* And he was asking her for help.

"Forget it." It was a struggle, but Kat kept her voice even. She handed the box back to him.

"I need you to hold on to it."

"No way."

"Seriously, Kat. This is a huge favor." He moved closer to her with the box in his hands, and she cringed against the door.

"I said no."

"Kat, listen. The stuff isn't mine. A guy owes me some money, and he gave me this as collateral, okay? It's worth a couple hundred bucks. But word on the street is that someone may have snitched on me to save his own ass. I want you to hold on to some of my money, too, in case I get searched. I don't want to have to explain where it came from." Mike reached into the deep pocket of his jeans and came up with a wad of bills. Big bills.

Kat's eyes searched his face. "What are you into, Mike?"

His eyes softened at the edges. "Come on, Kat." His voice was gentle, deep, warm. It brushed her face like soft fingers. "I'm asking for your help."

"I'm not holding on to drugs for you."

"Three days, that's all I need. This is no big deal."

"If it's no big deal, why are you dumping it on me?" Kat shot back. "Keep it in your own house."

"Nobody is going to be searching your place, okay?" Closing his eyes, Mike heaved a deep sigh. "Look, probably nothing is even going to happen. I just want to be careful." Reaching over, he touched Kat's hair, drawing his fingers against her scalp behind her ear. "You're the only person I trust right now."

"God, Mike." Kat hesitated, pressing her lips together. "What if Lala finds it?"

"Oh, come on. Lala would never go searching through your stuff. You don't have to touch anything inside the box. Just hide it well."

Kat didn't speak as he pressed the box into her hands. It felt cool under her palms.

"Three days," Mike said.

Kat looked into those eyes, as glittering as the sea. "I hate you," Kat told him.

Mike grinned. "I hate you, too," he whispered as he leaned over to kiss her.

✳✳✳

Jerrica walked past the door to the upstairs guest room, then stopped, hovering in the doorway.

"Do you need some help with that?"

Angela looked up from the plastic tray, thick with apple-green paint. She was wearing an ancient pair of jeans—acid wash, a complete relic—and one of Jerrica's father's old shirts. A blob of paint was caught in her brown curls, like a green snowflake. She blinked in surprise. "No," she said finally, holding her paint roller out in front of her. "No, thanks. I'm all right."

"You're dripping paint on your shoe."

"Dammit!"

Reaching for the wad of paper towels next to the tray, Jerrica snapped off a rectangle and handed it to her future stepmother. Cursing softly, Angela dabbed at her white Keds. Her formerly white Keds.

Jerrica looked around the mostly empty room. The double bed had been removed to the basement, along with two side tables, a small desk, an Oriental rug, and a tall wooden bookcase. The room looked smaller stripped of its furniture, but brighter. Blue painter's tape framed the wall with the two windows, and newspaper was laid unevenly on the floor. Unease washed through Jerrica. She felt as if the floor had suddenly shifted beneath her feet.

"Where are the prints?" Jerrica asked.

Angela frowned. "The...? I'm sorry..." She tucked a wayward lock of hair behind her ear, cocking her head. "Help me out here."

"Ancient Rome?" Jerrica prompted. "Black-and-white?" Jerrica's mother had collected them on her honeymoon.

"Oh, right, the etchings. Your father wanted them for his office."

Jerrica nodded, and Angela dipped her roller in the juicy green color. A few ribbons already swept uncertainly across the wall. "I don't know what made me think I could do this," Angela confessed. "I guess I've been watching too many home makeover shows."

As the two stood there facing each other, Jerrica wondered briefly what she looked like from where her future stepmother stood. A slim figure in black against the cheerful yellow of the guest room wall. A sliver of darkness.

"Actually...," Angela said after a moment, "I think I would like some help. If you don't mind."

"I don't mind."

A clean black-bristled brush lay beside the tray, and Jerrica dipped it into the green. She remembered the day she'd decided to paint her room dark red. She was surprised at how liberating it was to change the color of her walls. Midnight blue followed; then purple so dark that it looked black. She didn't mind the sour tang that burned the edge of her nostrils when she painted. In fact, she kind of liked it. The smell meant change. "I'll do the edges," Jerrica said. That was her favorite part of the job. A perfect role for a perfectionist.

"Don't you want to change your clothes?" Angela suggested.

Jerrica shrugged. "I like this color," she said of the green. It reminded her of five, a number that always gave her a happy feeling.

"Hmm." Angela turned to the wall and swept a stripe of green across its surface.

The room was silent except for the quiet hiss of the roller across wide stretches of wall. Jerrica finished one side, and Angela swept the roller up to the edges, blending the paint into a seamless single block of color. Jerrica smoothed paint around the corner of a window frame, consciously forming the number seven with her brush. *Seven is a lucky number,* Jerrica thought. It was lucky in many cultures—there were seven chakras in the Hindu tradition; Japanese Buddhists believed that people were reincarnated seven times; the Cherokee believed in seven levels of the universe; our own calendar had seven days of the week . . .

She wondered what Sanjay would think if she told him that she had secretly painted a seven onto the wall of the baby's room. She supposed that he would ask her if she really thought it might help.

When Jerrica finished the other side, she looked up to see that Angela was watching her, a slight smile on her face.

"What?" Jerrica asked, wondering if she had spilled paint on some part of herself that she couldn't see.

"You look so serious." Angela dipped her roller into the paint, then sent it gliding across the wall again.

"I do?"

"Very." She gave Jerrica a sidelong look, and Jerrica felt her ears burn. "Like painting this wall is some kind of problem for you to solve," Angela said.

Jerrica looked down at the tray of smooth paint. She touched the tip of her brush to the green and drew it across the lip of the tray. Then, carefully, she reached out to start on the second coat.

\*\*\*

The sun had disappeared behind the ragged line of mountains in the distance, but the edge of the sky was still deep gold with its light. Overhead, pink and purple clouds swirled together, disappearing into a deep blue-gray sea. All that beauty seemed wasted, set as it was over the endless line of boxy buildings—pet store, fast-food restaurant, Wal-Mart, coffee shop, supermarket, bookstore—and traffic lights. It was small wonder that Jerrica's father didn't even seem to notice the swirl of colors as he piloted his white Mercedes through traffic. He looked straight ahead, seeing only the cars around him and enough road to navigate by.

"So," Mr. Tyler said brightly as he steered around a creeping yellow Civic making a left turn, "Angela tells me that you were a huge help painting the nursery the other day." The side of his mouth curved into a proud smile.

"It was no big deal," Jerrica told him. She spotted the enormous stone dragons up the street, crouching on either side of the red lacquer door leading to Xiang, the Chinese restaurant where she and her father were meeting Angela.

"Well, it was a very big deal to Angela," Mr. Tyler said as he slowed to a stop at a red light. "She appreciated what you did."

Jerrica glanced at the green digital numbers on her father's dashboard. Seven-twenty-seven. By the time they pulled into the parking lot, they would be right on time. Seven-twenty-seven. Seven-twenty-seven. Twenty-seven. The numbers ticked across Jerrica's mind, repeating strangely. Violet with streaks of orange curved in a crazy patchwork across her mind, and a tornado of color screamed past her ears, deafening her; she couldn't catch her breath, she was drowning in geometric shapes . . .

Suddenly fear bloomed like fire in her belly. She pressed the lever to lower her window.

The light changed and her father's foot moved to the accelerator, but Jerrica's hand was faster. Reaching over, she pulled the key from the ignition.

The car behind them blasted a honk as her father shouted, "What are you—" Her father reached for the keys, but Jerrica had flung them out the window. "Dammit, Jerrica! What the hell are you—"

The blue sedan pulled around them, and at the next moment a red pickup truck screeched through the intersection in front of them, leaving long strips of rubber across the pavement. Metal crunched and glass shattered as the truck made contact with the sedan. Jerrica screamed, feeling the crash in her bones.

*Except she hadn't.*

Jerrica's father didn't move. "Oh my God," he whispered. A woman was already running toward the accident, dialing her cell phone.

Mr. Tyler's green eyes fastened onto his daughter's face. "Did you—how did you know—"

Jerrica's breath was coming in thin gasps. Her eyes were huge as she gaped at the scene in front of them. On the passenger's side, the blue sedan's door had been crushed. The passenger seat—the seat where she would have been—was vacant in the other car . . .

"Jerrica—" Her father reached over to touch her hair. "Jerrica.

You're okay. We're both okay." He put his hands on the sides of her face, forcing her to look at him. "We're okay," he said.

Jerrica leaned against the padded leather seat and closed her eyes, forcing herself to breathe in, breathe out. But behind her closed eyes, the accident was still there. Now the drivers were stepping—wobbly and uncertain—from their cars. The blue car was crushed on one side, but the truck had only minor damage.

*Because of me,* Jerrica thought. The realization seeped into her as if she were drinking it through her pores. *That should have been me. I was supposed to be in the path of the pickup.*

The violet-and-orange sunburst had receded in her mind, like a wave returning to the ocean.

She felt something shift deep in her DNA. The Principles had clicked and whirled into place. They had revealed that bit of the future and allowed her to adjust it.

This was the answer she had been looking for.

The Principles weren't just for gaming and math. They held the key to all events, all outcomes, throughout time.

Just as she thought—everything was connected.

***

"In the end, it wasn't a big deal," Sanjay said as he concentrated on catching a drip from his strawberry Popsicle. "They were very polite."

"That's not the point, Sanjay." Jerrica shook her head impatiently. They had just spent an hour and a half in a casino. The minute they were up by eight hundred dollars, a man in a gray blazer had walked over and quietly asked Sanjay to leave. "The point is that now they all know who you are." Jerrica knew that the casino security systems were linked, that they had face recognition technology to help them spot advantaged players. "Now they'll spot you wherever we go."

"So do you want to quit?" Sanjay's lips were stained pink, and Jerrica couldn't help thinking how sweet and silly he looked at that moment. "Is that what you're saying?"

"No." Air whooshed through Jerrica's nostrils in a determined exhalation. "I don't want to quit."

"Why not?" Sanjay asked. He scraped the last bit of Popsicle with his teeth, then tossed the stick into an overflowing garbage can. "I don't get you, Jerrica. Why are you even doing this? What's in it for you?"

The question took Jerrica by surprise. "You really don't know?" This whole time, she had assumed that Sanjay understood her project. And that it was about so much more than just money . . .

Jerrica narrowed her eyes to look down the street. Even in late afternoon, the sun was strong, and she wished she had thought to put a pair of sunglasses in her bag. This street was only three blocks off the Strip, but it was nearly deserted. Without the usual waves of tourists to dodge, it was much easier to talk. The sun was just setting, and the city was breathing a sigh of relief as a warm wind blew between the buildings and over the asphalt. "Think about the Heisenberg uncertainty principle," she said.

Sanjay nodded. "Okay."

Jerrica stopped, and a slow smile curved at the corners of her lips. "You don't know what that is, of course."

He thought about lying but decided it was pointless. "No clue," he admitted with a grin.

"Okay, it's basically the idea that you can never objectively observe anything." Jerrica searched his face, looking for a trace of understanding there. "Anytime you observe it, you change it."

Sanjay thought this over. "So we're affecting the games—"

"—by playing them." Jerrica nodded. "Right. Now, the question is: Can we affect them to our advantage? Why are some people lucky, while others get hit by lightning four times?"

Sanjay walked to a decrepit bench outside a run-down Mexican restaurant. It was six-fifteen, and only two solo diners were inside. Sanjay felt a strange wave of sadness for them as Jerrica sat down beside him. "Come on, you can't get struck by lightning four times."

"There was a major in the British army who was struck three times. Then lightning struck his tombstone. There's a park ranger in Virginia who has been struck seven times."

"Bizarre."

"Tell me about it." As Jerrica scratched at the bench's peeling brown paint with a grubby-looking fingernail, Sanjay couldn't help thinking—for the thousandth time—that she would be more than pretty if she just tried a little. *Maybe Kat could help her out?*

"Why would the same woman win the New Jersey lottery twice?" Jerrica asked after a moment. "The chances are in the millions that she would win it *once*."

"Coincidence?"

"What does that word even mean?" Jerrica sat back, blowing her straight bangs out of her eyes. "It means that the universe is meaningless."

"The universe *is* meaningless."

"No. No. It's just that we don't *understand* the meaning."

Sanjay thought that over. It was comforting, actually, to think that the things he did, his life, his choices—that all of that had some purpose. It was why people got into religion, he guessed. And even though he wasn't entirely sure that he believed it, he knew that he wanted to. "Do you think it's possible to stop being the guy who gets hit by lightning," Sanjay asked, "and become a lottery guy?"

"That's why I don't want to quit. It's about more than games, Sanjay. It's about life. It's about being in the world in a way that's . . . safe. Or better than safe."

She was looking at him with those green eyes, green as the deep sea. Who knew what mysteries lay in the depths? Monsters, maybe? Or beautiful phosphorescent treasures lost in the darkness? "How do you do it?" Sanjay asked.

"Do what?"

"Think the way you do."

Jerrica shook her head. "How does anyone think the way they think?"

"Other people's brains don't work the way yours does, Jerrica," Sanjay told her. "Believe me."

A gentle breeze breathed over them, lifting a strand of hair from the side of Jerrica's head toward her face. The black lock fell across her lips, and before he could think, Sanjay reached out, tucking it back into place with one long, sensuous finger.

Jerrica closed her eyes. When she opened them, slowly, she looked dreamy. *What thoughts are floating through your mind, strange girl?* Sanjay wondered. There was something about this girl that touched a very tender part of him. He imagined her as a tiny silver fish alone in a vast ocean, and he was surprised at how much he wished he could curl up around her, like the tendrils of an anemone, and protect her. "How close are you to figuring out if, you know, there's an equation for all of this?"

Confusion muddied her features for a moment, and then her dreamy expression snapped into focus. "Far," she said uncomfortably. *But why?* she asked herself. The main question was whether or not she could turn her intuition into math that others could use. *But if I ever succeed, Sanjay won't need me anymore.* It was the first time she had ever allowed herself to think that. "Professor Watkins has been working on the same problem for years. We may never figure it out."

"But you think you will."

Jerrica stared out at the clouds, thin ripples on the horizon. "I'm . . . hopeful." She peered up at him, the awe of her project clear in her expression. Sanjay didn't know any of this. He knew only that she looked the way he felt when he was playing, when he had cards in his hand or chips at his fingers. It was a mix of raw energy and power, fear and hope. Her expression made Sanjay feel that Jerrica understood him a little and that he understood a piece of her.

He smiled at her then. "So am I," he said.

Jerrica's heart gave an uncertain flutter, like a butterfly struggling to stay airborne. It had been a long time since she had felt so understood—so connected to someone. Were the Principles behind it, clicking and turning, moving the pieces into place? Had they ensured that she would meet this boy just as she became interested in games, in numbers?

Or was it something else?

Sanjay's eyes had been searching the ground, and when he looked up suddenly, Jerrica felt as if a spotlight was shining directly on her. "Look, Jerrica, if you're worried about getting caught again, we could bring in another player."

"Another player?"

"Sure. Look, I'm the one they've ID'd. If I start winning again, they'll spot me sooner or later. And—whatever happens—we don't want them to connect you to anything. If they ID you, the whole thing is history. You won't be able to go back there. So what we need is another player."

"I don't know . . . Who did you have in mind?"

"How about Kat?"

Jerrica shifted uncomfortably on the bench, as if her legs had fallen asleep. "Your girlfriend?"

"Yeah, she's my girlfriend." Sanjay laid his arm across the back of the bench. "And she's smart, and good at keeping secrets."

Jerrica hesitated, unwilling to admit just how squirmy the idea made her. The truth was, she had started thinking of Sanjay as . . . well, as *hers.* "I don't know . . ."

"I can't trust anyone else," Sanjay said.

"I don't trust anyone. Period."

"You trust *me,*" Sanjay pointed out. Jerrica looked at him, wondering if this was true. *But I must, in a way.*

And he was right—they needed a new player. The accident the day before had convinced her that she had to keep going. "Go ahead, ask her," she said.

Sanjay nodded. "Yeah." Honestly, he would have preferred to keep this thing between himself and Jerrica. At least until she handed over the contents of her notebook. But Sanjay sensed that she wasn't ready for that, and he wasn't about to force the issue.

*Maybe someday, but not yet.* He could wait. *As long as I keep winning.*

\*\*\*

"Hey, buddy." Tom Wilkins offered Sanjay a casual high five and he slapped it. "Where's Kat?"

Sanjay thought it was funny how everyone always asked him

where Kat was. He wondered if they did the same thing to her—demanded an explanation for every second of her aloneness. It was weird, when you thought about it. Especially since they had only been dating six months. And—really—just how well did you get to know someone in six months?

"I guess she's late," Sanjay replied, casting a glance over his shoulder toward the glass double doors.

"Eh," Tom said, with a shrug of his massive football shoulders. "Girls!" He tilted his head to the side, cracking his thick neck as a gaggle of freshman girls streamed past them toward the curb where parents were lined up, waiting to chauffeur them home. "You've got me down for the game Sunday—right, man?"

"Dude, you're down," Sanjay told him, giving him a punch on the shoulder. "Quit worrying."

"I'm gonna win big, dude." Tom pointed at Sanjay with a cocky smile. "You watch me."

"Not with that dumb-ass double-or-nothing bet," Sanjay shot back. Sanjay had started taking bets. He liked evaluating others' bets, calculating their odds. The payouts could be rough sometimes, but it was lucrative often enough.

"Just sit back and watch me." Tom clapped Sanjay on the shoulder. "Later."

Sanjay nodded as Tom disappeared into the gym entrance behind him. The sun was warm on his face, setting off a dull throbbing along his temple.

When Kat appeared, her first words to him were, "Where were you?"

"What?"

"The library?" Kat prompted. "We were supposed to hook up?" She was wearing a long white Indian shirt that fluttered around her legs and a pink tank top. To him, she looked like a sexy, pissed-off angel.

"Oh—that. Sorry, Kat. I guess I—" Sanjay shook his head. "Listen, Kat, I have to tell you about something."

Suddenly Kat felt as if she had swallowed an oyster—something cold and slimy settled into her chest. "Would this happen to involve Jerrica Tyler?"

"It's . . . it's not what you think," Sanjay told her.

"Why don't you just tell me?" Kat suggested, her voice flat and cold.

Sanjay shook his head. "It's just—what I'm going to tell you—it's very weird, and you can't tell anyone."

Kat's eyes traced the line of Sanjay's sharp profile as the brilliant sun beat down on his gleaming hair. He was handsome. Very. In fact, if one could ever be objective about these things, Kat would have had to say that she thought Sanjay was far handsomer than Mike. Two guys who were so different—and so similar, of course. Both smart. Both ambitious, in their own ways. *But Sanjay has a future, doesn't he?* "What is it, Sanjay?"

Sanjay pursed his lips. "Kat—I've been doing some . . . gambling." He turned to face her, and the intensity of his gaze was like a slap.

"Gambling," Kat repeated. She struggled to keep the emotion out of her voice. *Fucking gambling.* She knew most people wouldn't agree, but gambling bothered her as much as what Mike was into. More, maybe.

"We've got a system. And it works."

So many, many—so many damn times had she heard that same line before from her mother. Just before the electricity was shut off. Before they were evicted. "Systems never work, Sanjay."

"This one does." Sanjay took her hand, and she felt an eerie sense of calm until he said, "It really works, Kat. Jerrica figured it out. Well, actually, she's still figuring it out."

"You and Jerrica have been going to casinos together?" she spluttered, cocking her head. "That's why you wanted the ID?"

"It works,". Sanjay insisted, pressing her hand. "We've won thousands of dollars."

Kat felt as if she had walked into a dream. "Thousands . . ." An idea descended on her, heavy and hard as stone. Thousands of dollars. Money. So much money that you could go anywhere . . . "So what's the system?" Kat felt the words fall heavily from her lips.

"I don't exactly know," Sanjay admitted. "Jerrica claims it's a series of mathematical principles. Maybe that's true. Or maybe she's partly psychic."

Kat gave him a look.

"You don't believe it."

"Would you?"

Sanjay sighed. He remembered the first day he had noticed Jerrica—that day in Mr. Argent's class when she had been asking about cards. He remembered the intensity in her green eyes. It was like staring at part of himself. "It's working, Kat. It's . . . it's all coming true."

"Why are you telling me this?"

Sanjay swallowed hard. Out on the soccer field, the team was running drills. Cutting, running, kicking, sliding. It was March, and the weather in Vegas was perfect for soccer. Sanjay wished suddenly that he was out on the field with the other small figures in the blue-and-gold uniforms. He'd never been much of an athlete, but he felt the sudden urge to run. "It looks like they've ID'd me as advantaged."

"Shit, Sanjay."

"It's okay, nothing happened."

Kat's eyes drifted over his face in an effort to read his expression. "So now you have to stop, right?"

"Kat." Sanjay's voice was low as he lifted his eyes to meet hers. "I can't stop. Not now. I need more money. And Jerrica won't play by herself. She doesn't even want the money."

"That's insane." Kat looked so shocked that Sanjay laughed.

Jerrica liked the math. And Sanjay understood that. For her math was the same thing that money was for him. An equalizer. A balm. A suit of armor. A way to make life comfortable, predictable. "So we need a new player," he said.

"I don't know anything about gambling," Kat lied. *Except that it will ruin your life.*

"You just have to follow Jerrica's lead."

The idea sounded too good to be true, and in Kat's world anything that was too good to be true was a lie. But beneath her doubt, Kat felt something else . . . maybe hope?

"Why do you need to keep winning?" Kat demanded. "You say you've won so much money—well, where is it?"

Sanjay winced, thinking about the money. He'd only been even for about forty-eight hours before he had to raid the store's cash. First there had been his online habit. Then he had started taking some action—working as a bookie. A strictly small-time one, of course. But he'd had to pay out a few bets lately, and things had gotten a little tight. "Just . . . try it. I'll spot you the money."

"I thought you didn't have any."

Sanjay smiled ruefully. "I can get some."

"Jesus Christ."

"Kat, come on—just try it. For me?" Sanjay widened his eyes

and tilted his head slightly. The Look. "It could mean a lot of money for you."

Kat sighed. "I must be a complete idiot." *Why can't I just say no to these guys? But what would be the point of saying no this time?* she wondered. *This could be the answer for Lala and me . . .*

"You'll do it?" Sanjay asked.

Kat pressed her palm against her forehead. "Let's just get out of here, Sanjay," she said.

He smiled and took her hand, because he knew what she meant.

CHAPTER
TEN

t he noise, the colors—she couldn't breathe deeply enough. Kat
balanced against the edge of the table to keep herself upright.
*It's this damn dress,* she thought. Now that Sanjay had been ID'd,
the plan was to be as unidentifiable as possible.

To that end, Jerrica had rejected her normal borderline goth
style in favor of a pair of tailored black pants and a crisp white
shirt. She wore glasses and had fixed her hair in a low bun. Her
look said, *Young Marketing Assistant in Town for a Conference.*

Kat wore a low-cut red sleeveless dress and high-heeled sandals.
Her hair was a show-offy red, and her wild curls were loose around
her heavily made-up face. Her look said, *Just Dumped by My Boyfriend
and Out on the Prowl.* Kat just hoped she looked older, at least
twenty-one. Men were definitely giving her the eye.

At first Kat had worried about drawing attention. But Sanjay
had insisted that she wear the dress. "They'll be looking at you,"
he'd explained, "but they won't really see *you.* This is exactly the
right type of attention."

Still, every time the croupier—a heavyset African American

man in a purple-and-gold brocade vest—looked in her direction, she had to bite her lip to keep from flinching.

Sanjay hovered nearby, taking small-time losses at a blackjack table. He assumed that nobody would notice him as long as he didn't win, but he had on something of a disguise anyway—he wore rectangular glasses with heavy frames, and his hair was gelled back. His job was to keep an eye out for personnel who might be onto them. If he spotted anyone or anything suspicious, he'd give them a signal (a double cough), and they'd be out of there.

Jerrica placed her first bet, touching her thumb lightly against the double zero. Kat placed her bets and stood back as the croupier spun the wheel. The moment she had walked into the casino, she had smelled the stale, perfumed scent of her mother. Then Kat noticed a woman at a slot machine—she had Julia's blond hair and that same blank look. The image had hit her like a fist to the gut.

The wheel slowed enough so that Kat could see the numbers, then slowed again as the white marble skipped and hopped, trying to pick a place to rest. A vision of Mike flashed in her mind. She remembered the warm breath that had moved past his lips, and she could almost feel his fingers in her hair . . .

"Double zero," the croupier said.

Kat inhaled, and now the air finally seemed to penetrate her lungs. *I won?*

As she pulled the chips toward her, Kat felt lighter. Her hand was steady and she wanted to kiss the double zero. Quickly, Kat did the math. She would have had to work more than twenty-three hours to make this much money at the shoe store.

Jerrica shrugged slightly as Kat collected her chips. She didn't look up from the table, but Kat knew that the shrug was for her benefit. It said, *Now you know.*

Kat tapped the chip impatiently against the rim of the table. *Hurry up, Jerrica. Place our bet.*

She couldn't wait to slap her chips down on this felt.

\*\*\*

The moment Jerrica's finger drew across the number eight, Kat placed a corner bet just below it. Overhead, pink clouds painted against a pale blue sky sent a rosy glow over the gamblers. They were now in Vienna—the casino, that is—and it was the third casino they had hit that night. Low, careful bets had yielded over five thousand dollars at the Marble Palace and almost four thousand in the swirling chaos of the Emerald. Kat had been eager to leave the last casino. It was surrounded by a roller coaster. The mere knowledge that there were people screaming and falling as they rode the rails that ribboned around the building left her feeling unsettled.

But she kept her focus then and now, even as her pulse pounded through her body and she swayed on her feet. She could feel Sanjay watching from nearby and wondered how he was doing at the blackjack table. Kat watched intently as the ball landed in its bed.

"The winner is twelve," said the petite female croupier in a heavy Caribbean accent. "Twelve is the winner."

Jerrica's eyes narrowed, and she frowned as the croupier swept away their chips. She bit her top lip, and Kat imagined that she was fighting a string of curse words that threatened to spill forth all over the group gathered around the black-and-red wheel. But she didn't look at Kat, didn't give away that they knew each other. She simply gave her head a little shake—nothing more than a twitch, really—and then placed her next bet. Her chips were on the line below twenty-one, but her index finger traced the twenty-four.

Jerrica's system wasn't perfect. They had lost a few bets. But

Sanjay had run the numbers, and on a good night the system worked with about sixty percent accuracy. That left a lot of room to win. Sometimes Jerrica thought about the drop—the term the casinos used for the total amount of the bets on the table—and her heart ached. She felt sorry for all of them, every loser.

Kat could tell that Jerrica wasn't happy with that ratio, never would be. She wanted one hundred percent.

"Looks like roulette's your game," said a voice beside Kat's ear.

Kat looked up into a pair of almond-shaped black eyes. A handsome guy with dark skin was smiling at her. He was wearing a polo shirt and khakis—he looked like a college guy. Probably an athlete, judging by the toned muscles in his arms.

"I prefer games that don't require any skill," Kat told him.

The guy had an easy laugh that showed off his white teeth. "I like games I can win," he said.

Kat lifted her eyebrows just as the croupier announced twenty-four.

"Hey, look at that," the handsome guy said in admiration as a pile of chips moved across the table toward Kat. "But you didn't even get the right number."

"I was on the corner," Kat explained.

"Does that count?"

"Ask the chips," she teased. But when she turned back to the table, she saw that Jerrica had already placed her chips. *Shit*, Kat thought, glancing up. Jerrica was staring at the croupier with a face made of stone.

*All right, all right.* Kat looked at where Jerrica had placed chips. Below the six, on the corner between sixteen and twenty, and on the line above thirty. She had five chips in her hand—she was supposed to play three bets. Kat hesitated, half expecting Jerrica to reach out and point to a number. But it didn't happen.

"Place your bets," the croupier said.

Kat knew that she should probably skip the round...but wouldn't it look suspicious if she just stood there? *Just place a bet,* she told herself. *Anything.*

She put her small stack of chips on the seventeen.

"Betting five chips on one number?" the guy asked.

"Figured I'd go for broke," Kat told him, forcing a small laugh. Five hundred dollars down the drain—the realization hit her like a physical pain. She itched to reach out and snatch the chips back, but once the wheel began its spin, no one was allowed to touch the bets.

The wheel slowed, and Kat fought the impatience welling up inside her. *Just get it over with,* she thought. This was a wash—she wanted to get on to the next bet.

*Click, click, click.* The ball rattled like an irregular heartbeat.

"Seventeen is the winner," the croupier announced. "The winner is seventeen."

"Oh, shit," Kat whispered. Over seventeen thousand dollars.

Her new friend pounded her on the back. "You won!"

Behind Jerrica, Sanjay let out a violent cough. Then another.

Kat's heart dropped. That was the signal to get out of there. Jerrica had already vanished. Kat felt rooted to the spot. The chips—the croupier hadn't finished handing them out. She couldn't leave without the money. Quickly, she started scooping chips into her handbag.

"Excuse me, miss." A finger touched her lightly on the shoulder.

Kat's breath caught and her body went cold as she turned to face the tall blond man standing behind her. He wore a black suit and a red tie. He would have looked like a Ken doll if he wasn't so short.

*Say something. Say something. But what?*

Sanjay's warnings rang in her mind. "Don't let them take you anywhere," he'd told her. "Just walk away."

*But how can I walk away when I can't move?*

"Excuse me." The Ken doll gave her a winning smile. "But are you staying at this hotel?"

"No," Kat said quickly. It was as if the word suddenly set the rest of her body in motion—she started to move away.

"Wait a moment," the Ken doll said. "I'd like to offer you a suite."

"That's awesome!" the cute guy said, laughing again.

"Wh . . ." Kat shook her head. "What?"

The Ken doll pressed his palms together, giving her a slight bow. It struck Kat as an odd gesture. "We like our big winners to enjoy their stay," the man explained. He pulled a pad from the inside breast pocket of his jacket. Tearing off a white sheet of paper, he initialed the bottom and handed the paper to Kat. "Here's a voucher. Just turn it in at the front desk and they'll set you up."

"Thank you . . . ," Kat breathed. For the first time, she noticed that the manager was wearing a name tag. ANDREW CONNORS, it read. "Thank you, Mr. Connors."

"Not at all," he said. "Please ask for me personally if you need anything." With another Crest smile, he bowed again and walked away.

"This must be your lucky night!" the handsome college guy told Kat.

"Yeah." She looked at the voucher in her hand and the pile of chips still on the table. "I guess it is," she said.

***

Against the lights behind Sanjay's face at that moment, his disguise looked to Jerrica like exactly that—a disguise. His clothes belonged to someone older, flashier. "It's too hot out here," Jerrica declared.

"I don't know why she did that." Sanjay was bewildered, but also hurt. He looked at Jerrica with eyes as soft as melted chocolate.

*It was a coincidence,* Jerrica wanted to explain. She knew that Kat hadn't seen her signal. "I don't know, either," she said instead. Then, with a flash of guilt, she added, "Do you think we should be worried?"

"About Kat? No way. She can take care of herself." But Sanjay ran a hand through his hair, so Jerrica knew that he was worried.

"I hope."

"Maybe we should go somewhere else?" Sanjay suggested.

"Like where? Most of the security systems are linked."

"Not to the reservations." Sanjay held her gaze.

"I will not take money from Native Americans." Jerrica tugged primly at the crisp white cuff of her sleeve, which glowed greenish in the lights from the casinos behind them.

"What are you talking about?"

"These casinos are just corporate icons, Sanjay." Jerrica tipped her chin at the various casinos that lined the Strip. "I don't want to take money from tribes of people who actually need it."

"Foxwoods is the biggest casino in the world!" Sanjay countered. "They have more money than they know what to do with."

"Isn't it in Connecticut?"

"Well . . . yeah."

"How am I supposed to explain being away that long to my dad?"

"Tell him you're a finalist in the national spelling bee."

Jerrica felt the tense muscles in her face melt into a smile. She shook her head. "You're nuts."

"National mathlete roundup?" Sanjay's eyes danced—he was teasing, of course.

Jerrica smirked. "Marginally more believable. But still no."

They were silent for a moment.

"So—what?" Sanjay asked. "Do you want to quit?"

"I can't. Not until the Principles are perfect." The longer Jerrica lived with her talent, the more frustrated she grew. The ability to see the numbers was starting to make her feel lonely—she just wished she could share the burden, even a little ... Being with Sanjay helped. "I can't quit."

"Me either." Turning, Sanjay looked down over the lip of the wall. *She can't quit. I need those equations.* For now, it was fine to just tag along and let Jerrica work her magic. But in the end, what he really wanted was to be able to do the magic himself.

Amid the mad rush and swirl, a heavyset woman pushing a stroller caught his attention. Her husband was filming the lights around them with his video camera. "Why do people bring their children to Las Vegas?"

"Because they're idiots." Jerrica's reply was as quick as a reflex kick.

"No." Sanjay looked at her face, at the changing lights that glowed on her pale skin. "Really."

"Maybe ... ," Jerrica said after a moment. "Maybe they're just chained to them. Even when they're trying to have a wild time." His lips were by her ear. His warm breath sent a tickle down her neck. Jerrica turned her face to him.

"Guys!"

They jumped apart, as if hit by an electric shock. Kat was hurrying through the crowd, weaving her way around a couple in matching T-shirts. She found her way over and grabbed Sanjay's hand. "They comped me a room!" she said breathlessly.

Sanjay gaped for a moment, but at Kat's eager smile, he started to laugh. "A room?" He looked at Jerrica.

Jerrica took a deep breath in an attempt to control her heartbeat. *They're going to go off together...*

"A suite!" Kat held up a voucher.

"Let's see." Jerrica took the voucher. She kept her movements quick so Kat wouldn't notice the waver in her hand. On the voucher was a photograph of the casino lit up at night, like a monster creeping out of the dark. Turning, she noticed an older man watching them, listening in on their conversation. He looked like a typical senior citizen tourist, but still, an inchworm of doubt crawled up Jerrica's spine. "Listen, let's get out of here," she said in a low voice.

She led the way down a long flight of stairs and took a quick left at the corner. They walked briskly, not speaking, for two blocks, until they were well off the Strip. Once they were far enough away for the lights to have subsided, Jerrica felt a bit more normal.

After three more blocks, they slowed down.

"Kat, let me take your chips," Sanjay said, pulling open his black messenger bag. She tossed in her chips, which clicked against the others Sanjay had in the bag.

"They just said that I should stay and have a good time."

"They want you to lose your money back to them," Sanjay said dryly.

"In most cases, a smart strategy," Jerrica added. "So—what are we going to do?"

Sanjay thought for a moment. "Well," he said at last, "I guess we should have a party."

"And attract *more* attention?" Jerrica demanded.

"Shouldn't we at least check it out?" Kat asked.

"But they can't know we're together," Jerrica insisted.

"Well—they can't know we're with *you*," Kat shot back. "Sanjay and I could go."

Jerrica looked at Sanjay, her heart beating double time. The idea of him taking off for a hotel room with Kat . . .

He just stared at the paper voucher.

"Sanjay's the one who's been spotted," Jerrica said after a moment. "He's the one who's been ID'd. If they realize you're with him . . ."

Kat nodded. "You're right." She took back the voucher and looked at it sadly. "It just seems like such a waste, doesn't it? Too bad we can't get some money for it."

"Oh, well." Sanjay turned to look at Jerrica with large eyes, then plucked the voucher from Kat's hand and placed it in the black messenger bag.

Jerrica was too overwhelmed even to notice the car pull up to the curb beside them. She snapped into the moment at the screech of the tires. Footsteps pounded. Two guys—one was tall, in a black hooded sweatshirt and jeans, and one was small and thick, like a fire hydrant—ran toward them.

Kat stumbled backward as the tall one reached for Sanjay's bag. Jerrica screamed and hit the guy in the shoulder.

"Quit it, bitch," the short one said, shoving her away. Jerrica was surprised by his strength. As she hit the pavement, her wrist twisted; the heel of her palm was skinned raw.

Sanjay gripped the handles of the bag, but the tall guy smashed him in the temple with a short piece of pipe. Blood poured through Sanjay's fingers as he touched the wound. The short guy landed a vicious kick to Sanjay's stomach. Sanjay doubled over, sinking to the pavement and finally letting go of the bag.

"Game's over," the short one said, and then they disappeared into the car with the bag. The tan sedan turned a corner before Jerrica could look at the license plate.

"Sanjay?" She heard the panic in her own voice as she crawled toward the place where Sanjay lay in a heap, gasping for air. "Jay!"

Sanjay let out a low groan. Pain throbbed at the side of his head, and he felt as if his face had been ripped in two. "I'm okay," he managed to say.

"You're not." Jerrica looked up at Kat, who was standing to the side, shivering like someone had just airlifted her from a glacier. "Call 911," Jerrica yelled to her.

Kat reached for her purse, but Sanjay said, "No." He shook his head. "Don't. I'm fine."

Kat's delicate thumb hovered over her phone, ready to dial, but she was staring at Jerrica. "What should I—"

"No cops," Sanjay said. "Are you insane?"

Jerrica pulled a packet of tissues from her purse. She struggled with the plastic wrapper, tearing it off and tossing it away before she pressed a wad of tissues to the side of Sanjay's face. "Can you sit up?"

Sanjay struggled to sit upright as the blood soaked into the tissues.

"We have to get you to a doctor," Jerrica said, inspecting the wound.

"Is it bad?" Sanjay asked.

"No." Actually, the cut wasn't as deep as she'd feared. Sanjay was going to have a nasty bruise, though.

He looked up into her eyes. "Oh, thank God," he said. "My beautiful face . . ." A slight smile curled the edges of his mouth.

"Not funny," Jerrica told him.

Sanjay struggled to his feet, and Jerrica helped him. "No," he said. "Not funny."

"We should still go to the emergency room," Kat said. Her eyes were huge and her cheeks were pale. She looked sick, like she might vomit. *As if she'd spent too much time on the merry-go-round,* Jerrica thought. "We don't have to tell them what happened, Sanjay, but someone has to look at your face."

Sanjay winced at the blood-soaked tissues. "All right," he said at last.

"How much was in the bag?" Jerrica asked. She knew that he'd been planning to cash out some chips.

Sanjay sighed. "A lot," he admitted.

"It doesn't matter," Jerrica said quickly. "We'll get it back." She snaked her arm around his shoulders, half to hold him up and half to feel the weight of his body. She had to assure herself that he was real, that he existed, that he was all right.

Sanjay smiled after a moment, but it felt forced. "Yeah, it's okay," he said. Although it wasn't, not one bit. *Who were those guys?* he wondered.

And deep inside Jerrica, something shivered. Why hadn't she seen this coming?

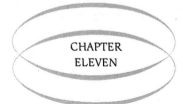

CHAPTER
ELEVEN

"god, I hate these places," Kat said, looking around at the mauve-cushioned wooden chairs, the round plastic tables shaped like cylinders, the gray industrial tile.

"Waiting rooms?" Jerrica asked.

"Hospitals." Kat folded her arms across her chest, shuddering slightly. She imagined a three-year-old Lala beside her, her palm blistered with a third-degree burn. Lala had reached for the pan on the stove. When Julia caught her, she reasoned that her daughter needed to understand that stoves were hot. So she held Lala's hand over the open gas flame. Just for a moment. Just enough for her to learn . . .

"Yeah." Jerrica nodded. "Me too." Her eyes turned blankly toward the floor-to-ceiling windows that lined one wall of the waiting room. Kat could see their reflections, like ghosts, in the glass. For a moment, she just watched herself, wondering what she was doing there.

Nearby, a young boy was sitting with his parents. He had tissues stuck up both nostrils and was tilting his head back while his mother stroked his arm. An older woman sat diagonally across from them, beneath a large poster of a red sunflower. She leaned on her cane, breathing shallowly with her eyes closed. She wore a lavender dress and one brown shoe. The other foot was swollen and stuck awkwardly out of a fuzzy yellow slipper.

Kat had gone with Sanjay when the triage nurse called his name. But when he went in to see the doctor, she'd stayed behind, not wanting to watch him get stitches.

A gurney rolled down a lit hall. A woman was lying on it, her belly huge beneath a pale blue blanket.

"Nobody ever gets well here," Jerrica said suddenly.

Kat turned to look at her. "Sure they do."

Jerrica blinked at Kat as if she weren't sure what they were talking about. "They do?"

There was something in Jerrica's face that reminded Kat of Lala when she was very small. Kat took her hand. "Sanjay's going to be okay."

Surprised at the warmth of Kat's palm, Jerrica looked down at their hands. She tried to jettison the image of her mother, pale and exhausted, in the white hospital bed. The first time, after Isabel was born—the baby had looked so tiny and horrible, covered in wires in a plastic box. And the second time. The second time, three months after Isabel had died, when Jerrica's mother was in the accident . . . She was in the hospital for four days, but she never got better. Finally, her heart just gave up, as if it had really, truly broken, like in a fairy tale . . .

Kat pulled Jerrica close to her, wrapping her arm lightly around Jerrica's shoulder. "Don't worry," she whispered. "It's all going to work out."

Jerrica closed her eyes and leaned her head against the flat place just below Kat's collarbone. But she couldn't believe Kat. A raw, aching fear had settled in her chest, like an intruder that would never leave.

A dark silhouette sliced its way into the pale box of light reaching in from the hallway. Kat released her arm and Jerrica sat up.

"Sorry to make you wait," Sanjay said. He smiled a little, then winced at the pain.

"How are you feeling?" Kat asked as Sanjay eased himself into the chair beside hers.

Sanjay pointed to the cross-hatching at the side of his face, half an inch from his left eye. "Does it make me look tough?"

"Like Frankenstein," Kat told him. "What are you going to tell your parents?"

"That I fell off my bike," Sanjay said smoothly.

"Do you even own a bike?" Jerrica asked.

"Quit bogging me down with technicalities. Okay, I'll tell them that I fell off of a friend's skateboard," Sanjay amended. "Then my mother can cluck and disapprove of how Americans never watch over their children."

Kat nodded. "Play to the bias. It always works." Her eyes lingered on the ugly red ladder. If it had been just a bit over, he could have lost an eye . . .

"Isn't it weird that we would be so lucky and so unlucky all in one night?" Sanjay said.

Kat stared at him for a moment, then cast a sideways glance at Jerrica, whose black brows were drawn darkly over her green eyes.

"Do you think," Jerrica asked, "that what happened was just a coincidence?"

"Yes," Kat said quickly.

Leaning back in his chair, Sanjay let out a heavy sigh. "Jerrica doesn't believe in coincidence."

"How much was in the bag?" Jerrica asked.

"Not sure," Sanjay admitted. He'd intended to give the bag to his contact. Now that he'd been ID'd, it would have been nearly impossible for him to cash out their chips. And Kat couldn't have done it all by herself—it would have taken too long, cashing in a couple hundred here, another five hundred there. He'd gotten the name of a consolidator, someone who was willing to buy the chips off of him for a cut of ten percent. Sanjay needed the money. And now he didn't have it.

"What are we going to do now?" Kat asked.

Jerrica sighed. "I don't know," she said. "I'm tired."

Sanjay reached across Kat to touch Jerrica's knee. "Hey," he said. "Hey—it's fine. It's no big deal—"

"I just don't think I want to do this anymore, Jay," Jerrica said. It was hard for her to say, but it was the truth. The futility of what she was doing had finally occurred to her. The Principles seemed further away than ever. Besides, if she ever succeeded in figuring them out, she would lose Sanjay. And if she didn't figure them out, she'd lose him anyway—in the end. *I never really had him to begin with,* she thought. *I was just kidding myself. He's with Kat.* "I'm tired," she repeated.

"But hey—hey, listen—" Sanjay started to say, but Kat placed a hand on his shoulder.

"She said she's *tired,*" Kat said. Sanjay's gaze met hers, but she didn't blink. "Give it a rest, okay?"

Sanjay sat there for a moment. He stared at the dark gray tile, his heart slamming against his rib cage. *Is Jerrica saying that it's over? It can't be. Not yet.* But he didn't dare push her.

"You guys can talk it over later, okay, Sanjay?" Kat said. She pressed against him slightly, so that his hand fell from Jerrica's knee.

Sanjay nodded. "Sure. No problem." His voice was a little too bright, too eager, but he did his best to cover that with a smile. "Hey—let's get out of here, okay? It's getting late, and my parents will freak if I'm not home by eleven." As he stood up, he realized that every inch of his body was aching. Even his eyelids hurt. *I'm just tired,* he told himself. *We'll all feel better after we get some rest . . .*

When Kat held out her hand, Jerrica took it, pulling herself out of the chair.

*She looks so pale and so small,* Sanjay thought. *Kat was right. She looks exhausted. Really, I'm glad she didn't let me push her. Jerrica could go right over the edge. With both feet.* He wanted to put a reassuring arm around her, to tell her that everything would be all right. But that seemed too strange with Kat standing there.

"Let's go home," he said.

***

The lights were on in the kitchen when Sanjay arrived. He'd briefly considered coming in through the front door, but he'd still have to pass the kitchen on the way to his room. Nobody ever used the front door.

He said a silent prayer in the hope that he would find his sister sitting at the bright yellow table. His fingers hovered over the doorknob, and he formed a complete mental image of Priya, her hair tucked into a messy bun at the nape of her neck. He imagined half a torn chapati and the remnants of that night's dinner on a plate in front of her. The good student's midnight snack.

The image had been so vivid that he was surprised to find his mother seated at the table. A large mug of peppermint tea sat before her, and she barely lifted her eyes when Sanjay walked through the door. "You're late," she said.

"I know," Sanjay admitted. This scenario was exactly why he and Jerrica had been doing most of their gaming in the afternoons—less explaining to do.

Sanjay walked to the cupboard and pulled out a tall glass. He held the glass under the tap, let the water foam into it, and took a long drink. The water offered a sweet relief.

"What happened to your face?" Sanjay's mother asked. "Were you fighting, Sanjay?"

Sanjay set the glass down. "Yeah, Ami," he said.

As he turned to face her, Mrs. Patel tucked one hand below her elbow and touched the other palm to her cheek.

Sanjay heard the water drip slowly from the tap. His father had been meaning to replace the washer for weeks, but he never got around to it.

In the dim light of the energy-saving fluorescent, Sanjay could detect long lines stretching from his mother's eyes to her temples. She wore a salmon-pink shalwar kameez—her favorite nightclothes. But the color made her skin look sallow and tired.

Sanjay was filled with a sudden urge to comfort his mother. He sat down across from her. "Ami, it's not a big deal," he said. "I just got into a stupid argument, that's all."

"That's *all*?" Mrs. Patel's gaze was challenging. "Is this how we raised you? You solve your problems with your fists?"

"I didn't *start* anything. I was just defending myself," Sanjay insisted. This, at least, was true.

"I don't think I want to know anything more." His mother held up her hand, with its long, elegant fingers so much like his own. "Your father fired David today."

"What? Why?" For a moment, Sanjay held out hope that his

father simply didn't want to pay for a night manager on weekends anymore. That he planned to work all the shifts himself . . .

"Because he discovered some discrepancies in the accounting." She held his gaze for a long moment, and Sanjay heard the slow, steady drip . . . drip . . . drip from the sink.

"How—how did he . . . ?"

His mother wrapped her fingers around her mug. "He wanted to surprise me," she said. "He wanted to take out enough money for a wedding gift, like I'd asked him. But when he checked, the numbers were off by more than two thousand dollars."

"I can return the money," Sanjay said.

As his mother shoved her chair away from the table, it made a horrible scraping sound across the linoleum. "What's done is done, Sanjay," his mother said. "But if that money isn't back in the bank by the weekend, I will tell your father everything. And you will never take another dime from our store. The only reason I haven't told him yet is because I know it would break his heart." Her voice caught, and her eyes sparkled with unshed tears. "No one else will suffer because of what you've done, do you understand?"

Sanjay felt his throat closing. "Ami, I'm sorry—"

"Just fix it," his mother hissed. Slowly, she stood up, padded to the sink, rinsed her cup, and placed it in the wooden rack to dry. She gave the cold water knob an extra twist, but a fat silver drop fell from the tap. Before she left the room, she looked at Sanjay as if she wasn't sure who he was anymore. He shrank under her gaze.

"I'll get the money," Sanjay promised as the question *How? how? how?* sang softly in his mind.

***

The guard studied Kat's identification, made a note on his clipboard, and then waved her through the gate and into the courtyard.

Her head felt muddy and dense as she walked into the austere visiting room.

She took a seat at a table. Around her, families buzzed and gathered, waiting for their loved ones. *Do any of them want to scream, run, escape? Are any of them afraid?*

The minute hand reached a quarter past the hour and the prisoners filed in. A broad, squat woman waiting near Kat burst into a huge smile at the sight of her husband. A riotous family swelled into a cacophony of voices at the appearance of a slender woman with ebony skin. But the beautiful blond woman with the perfect posture didn't even look around as she strode in at the end of the column. Kat had to wave to get her attention.

When she saw Kat, Julia's slender eyebrows flickered. Without makeup, Kat's mother looked vulnerable, almost ghostly. There was a faint white scar at her temple, the only remaining visible sign from the night of the accident. Her stride was purposeful as she walked. Straight as a stick. She slid into the chair across from Kat's.

For a long moment, they just looked at each other.

Finally Julia spoke. "Thought you'd come sooner." Her voice sounded tinny and strange.

"I'm sorry," Kat said, instantly regretting it. Her mother hated those words. Kat then muttered something about being busy with school, but Julia cut her off with a wave of the hand.

"It doesn't matter," she said. "Where's Lala?"

"She couldn't make it," Kat replied quickly.

"A ten-year-old girl is too busy to visit her mother?"

"I wanted to talk to you alone."

Julia spread her hands on the table, palms down, fingers splayed wide. "You got the letter."

"I got it."

"The lawyer says it would really help my case if you could show up at the hearing," Julia said. "Lala too." She leaned forward. "I could be out of here in two months," she hissed.

*Two months.* All Kat had to do was show up at the parole hearing and talk about how much she missed her mother, what a great parent she was, how she was sure that Julia felt deep remorse . . .

Julia smiled. "Remember all the fun we used to have, Kitten? Remember the time we went to the carnival and you ate two cones of cotton candy and how—"

"—the man let us ride on the teacups as long as we wanted?"

Men were always giving Julia special attention. The memory, long buried, rose up again, making Kat dizzy.

"It'll be like that," Julia promised.

Her mother could be fun, unpredictable, impulsive. But Kat also thought about the endless string of boyfriends—all the creeps and crazies. And she remembered the time Julia had a lock installed on the outside of Lala's door so that she could keep her from wandering into the kitchen at night. And the time she kept Lala in her room for twenty-four hours because she had spilled grape juice on Julia's favorite shirt. She thought about the things her mother told her—that she was a liar, a pig, a selfish beast, a bitch, worthless. She thought about all of the things that her mother could have done to protect them but didn't, or wouldn't, do.

*Maybe jail is the best place for her. For us. For me.*

Right now, Kat didn't have enough money to take Lala and get out of town. But she could. If Jerrica would help . . .

Reaching out, Julia touched Kat's hand. "Don't forget, Kat," she said. "Don't forget how it could be."

*She's still so beautiful,* Kat thought. *Hard and fierce—like a lion. No—a liar.*

"I miss you. I miss Lala." Tears sparkled in Julia's eyes, and Kat felt a familiar tug at her chest. As if she could forget about the hit-and-run that put Julia in prison for almost two years.

Kat had been half asleep in the recliner, watching TV, when her mother raced in, wild-eyed and frightened. It was three in the morning, but Kat was fifteen years old, and whenever her mother disappeared for the night she would stay awake, watching the door. Twice before, she had stayed awake for forty-eight hours, waiting.

The minute her mother burst through the front door, adrenaline zinged through Kat's body. "What happened?" Kat asked, but Julia just brushed past her, went to the kitchen, and poured herself some vodka. She stood over the sink, staring at the window. It was dark out, and Kat wasn't sure if her mother was looking into the night or watching her own reflection in the glass.

Kat stood in the doorway for a moment, silent as a stone. "Mom?" Kat asked.

Julia turned to face her. "You were with me in the car," she said.

"What?"

"There was an accident," Julia said. "Oh, God." She covered her eyes with her hands. "I think I killed him."

Kat's stomach dropped. But at the same time, it was as if she had always expected this to happen. "What?" she whispered.

"Kat, listen to me." Julia crossed the black-and-white linoleum in two steps and gripped her daughter's shoulders with iron fingers. She leaned down slightly so that her eyes were level with Kat's. "There was an accident," Julia said, "and I drove away. This man, I don't know where he came from. I guess he was trying to cross the street—it was dark, I—" Julia's eyes glittered, wet. Her nose turned pink and began to run. Kat could smell her liquory breath.

"Did anyone see?" Kat was amazed—horrified—that she had asked this question.

Julia nodded grimly. "Maybe. There were a couple of people at the intersection. Still, it was dark . . ." Her fingers tightened on Kat's shoulders, and Kat winced under their pressure. "If anyone finds out," Julia said, "I'll tell them that you were in the car with me—that you were hysterical and I thought you were hurt. I'll say I took you home right away to take care of you." Julia used her wrist to wipe away the clear fluid that streamed from her left nostril. "We'll say that Mrs. Jennett was watching Lala."

Mrs. Jennett was their neighbor, and she sometimes babysat when Julia remembered to ask her. She was old, though; ancient and stooped with age. She often got her days mixed up.

"You're the only one I can count on," Julia whispered, pulling her daughter into a hug. "Kat, you have to help me."

Kat could smell the warm scent of her mother's hair, the faded notes of her perfume. "I'll help you, Mom," she promised.

The police arrived the next day. A witness had remembered a partial license plate, they explained. Kat repeated the story exactly as her mother had told it, and the police arrested Julia. Kat had sat down with a heavyset woman in a bright green suit who turned out to be a social worker. Anita Maple was her name, and she was the one who called Trish and eventually assigned her temporary custody.

It turned out that Julia hadn't killed the man. But she had broken his leg and fractured his ankle. He would recover fully. Still, the minimum sentence in a hit-and-run was two years. When Julia told her story—the story of a panicked mother desperate to make sure her daughter was all right—the district attorney had offered a plea agreement. Two and a half years in the Nevada Women's Correctional Facility; possibly less with good behavior. Julia took it.

There was never even a trial.

Kat had told the false version of that night so many times that eventually she started to wonder what had actually happened.

Julia looked around the visiting room, her mouth pursing slightly as she stared at the green linoleum floor. "I can't wait to get out of here," she spat. Those were the first words that Kat believed.

"I'm sorry," Kat said, cringing.

"Don't say that!" Julia snapped. "Don't ever say that! *I'm* not sorry. I'm here, I did my time." She sucked in her cheeks, setting her jaw. "I just can't wait for us to be together again. To be a family." Her blue eyes searched Kat's face, and Kat wondered what she saw there. *Do I look like a stranger to her?* Kat wondered. *As much like a stranger as she looks to me?*

"Me too," Kat said.

They sat for a few moments more. When the guard announced that time was over, Julia gave Kat's hand a final squeeze. "You'll be there?" she said, but it was only partially a question.

"I'll be there," Kat promised.

Now she was the liar. *Like mother, like daughter.*

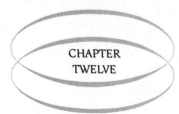

CHAPTER
TWELVE

"**G**ive me that," Sanjay said, plucking the cigarette from his sister's fingers. He inhaled deeply, as if it might resuscitate him.

"You don't even smoke," Priya pointed out, reaching for the cigarette.

Sanjay waved her off. "Today I do."

"Girl problems?"

"Is it that obvious?" Sanjay glanced up at the no-entry sign over the rear door of the shop. Priya had propped it open with a broom handle.

She leaned against the brick wall, wearing a slight smirk. "What else?"

Sanjay coughed slightly and cast a frown at the cigarette. "God, this is disgusting. You've got to cut this out."

Priya shrugged. "Eh. I only smoke a half a pack a day."

"That's a lot."

"It isn't crack, Sanjay."

"Now, there's looking on the bright side. By the way, your break's over. Dad needs you to restock the items." Sanjay grinned.

"Why don't you do it?"

"I'm done."

"You're cutting out early? You jerk."

"Hey, I've been working weeknights."

Priya smoothed an apron over her bulky body. "Don't talk to me." She pulled a breath mint out of her pocket and popped it into her mouth, then spritzed herself with cologne.

"Everyone knows you smoke, Priya," Sanjay told his sister.

"That doesn't mean I want to rub it in their faces," she shot back. "Oh, look—here comes trouble now." An ancient, beat-up blue Ford steered into the rear parking lot and pulled into a space near the recycling shed that Sanjay had built with his father. It was Kat's aunt's car. "Good luck," Priya singsonged; then she pranced back inside.

Kat stepped out of the car and stood behind the open door for a moment, almost wearing it as a shield. She just stood there, watching, as Sanjay put the cigarette in his mouth and unfastened his apron. He pulled it off, reflexively rolling it up into a neat cylinder and wrapping the long strings around it. Taking a final puff, he tossed the butt away. Smoke trailed from his nostrils as he walked toward Kat. "Hi," he said.

"Hi." Kat's voice was low and cautious. "You wanted to talk?"

"Yeah."

Kat stepped out from behind her car door, slamming it closed. There was something about the solidity of a door closing behind her that she found comforting. Once things were closed, you could leave them behind. Move on. "Let's walk."

The strip mall backed up on a park—just a few basketball courts and a play area for little kids. The place was deserted today, which was a relief to Sanjay as he sat on the faux-wood gray plastic bench beside Kat. The sun was starting its descent, casting pink fingers across the sky.

"There's something I need to tell you."

Kat nodded. She had never seen him look so serious.

Sanjay wiped his hands on his jeans and looked at her sharply. "Kat—I need to borrow some money." He winced, as if the words hurt him.

"I—" Kat was suddenly overwhelmed. She felt as if she had fallen into a deep, deep hole. "I need money, too. Actually, I'm freaking out a little."

Sanjay put his head in his hands. "We have to talk to Jerrica."

"But we'll still need some money to start up," Kat pointed out. "I've only got a little—a hundred fifty."

Sanjay shook his head. "Too little," he said. That was the thing—Jerrica didn't always get a vision. If she lost a few in a row, they would be out of luck.

They sat there for a moment, both staring off toward the empty swing set. A dry breeze blew, and one of the black plastic swings moved forward an inch on the chains that held it in place.

"Can't you ask your parents for money?" Kat asked.

Sanjay barked a laugh that was more final than any no.

"Okay." Overhead, the clouds were lit with the sun's golden fire at the edge of the horizon as the sun set behind the playground. Its beauty burned against Kat's eyes so that when she closed them, the scene flashed silver against the darkness. There was a solution to this problem. One that came with its own set of problems—Mike's fat wad of bills, still sitting in a corner of her closet. It was well after the time he said he'd be back to collect it. *Has to be at least a thousand dollars.*

The window of opportunity was closing . . .

"Will you talk to Jerrica?" Kat asked.

"I'll talk to her."

She looked at Sanjay carefully—his beautifully formed mouth, those full lips. "She said she didn't want to go to any more casinos."

Sanjay looked down at his palms. "We'll see."

"Okay." Kat stood up, brushing her hair out of her eyes. "I know where I can get some money."

***

"I wasn't sure anyone was home," Sanjay said as the pretty brunette woman opened the door. She tilted her head slightly, her look questioning, and Sanjay searched her face for signs of Jerrica. He thought he saw a hint there at the jaw, but he wasn't sure.

"I was in the kitchen," the woman said, by way of explanation. "Can I help you?"

"I'm a friend of Jerrica's—" Before he could finish, Jerrica appeared at the woman's side. Inside, the house was silent and dark. Jerrica's pale face was nestled in her black hair, round and fragile as a dandelion turned to seed. His heart gave an unexpected trip at the image—he half expected her to blow away at the slightest breath. He cleared his throat. "Hey."

"Hey," she said. She turned to the pretty woman. "Angela, this is Sanjay."

Angela flashed a huge smile, as if the name meant something to her, and lifted her eyebrows at Jerrica. "Well, then," she said, clearing her throat. "Well, I guess I'll just go check on dinner. Really nice meeting you, Sanjay." Angela scurried across the red-and-blue Oriental carpet that covered the oak floor in the wide living room and disappeared through a doorway. Sanjay wondered briefly what it would be like to sink into that leather sofa.

Jerrica looked tired, and Sanjay worried that he had woken her up. *Maybe she was taking a nap?* "Look, uh—Jerrica . . ." He wasn't sure where to go from there. They'd had a plan to meet after school that day, but Jerrica had never shown up. That made him nervous. "Do you want to go for a walk?"

"Okay," Jerrica said. As she stepped outside, her heart gave a familiar flutter. She pulled the door shut. It was still hot, but not uncomfortably so. It was almost a relief for Jerrica to feel the warm air on her skin. Her house was so over-air-conditioned. Frigid.

As they stepped onto the walkway, Sanjay noticed that Jerrica was barefoot. The sun had dipped below the horizon, and the neatly swept concrete pavement would be just comfortably warm against her soles. *When you think about it,* Sanjay mused, *there really isn't much reason to wear shoes in a neighborhood like this.* There was no gum to stick to your feet, no broken bottles, not even a bit of stray gravel. You were perfectly safe.

"How's your face?" Jerrica asked.

"The stitches itch, but it doesn't hurt much."

"That's good," Jerrica said. They walked for a few moments in silence. It was strange, Jerrica thought, to be walking around in her own neighborhood. It made her realize that she usually only passed through it in her father's car. She admired the palm trees that towered over the white adobe-style house at the end of the block. The red roof was beautiful against the slowly purpling sky.

"Jerrica . . . I need to ask you a question."

She looked at him sharply, and Sanjay hesitated. These things needed to be built up to, Sanjay knew. So he simply said, "Is everything okay with you?"

Jerrica tensed. There were many ways to interpret and answer that question, but what she chose was, "Of course."

They turned a corner and came to the edge of a green park. At the center was a man-made lake surrounded by palm trees. *Fake but beautiful,* Jerrica thought.

"Was that your mother?" Sanjay asked, just to have something to say.

"My mother's dead."

Sanjay was struck dumb for a moment. *How could I not have known that?* he wondered. It was as if a chink had appeared in a wall, flooding his face with an insistent light. "I'm sorry," he said.

"Everyone says that," Jerrica told him. "And I have no idea what to say back." She looked down at the greenish water. They were at the edge of the lake now, and Jerrica could see the bright algae that had collected at the swampy edges.

"How did she die?"

"Car accident," Jerrica said.

"Oh." Sanjay looked pained. His dark eyes were like deep wells. Jerrica felt herself falling into them.

*He may not know everything about me,* Jerrica thought, *but he knows parts of me.*

Sanjay gently touched her arm—tentatively, the way you might stroke a kitten that hadn't yet opened its eyes. His fingers were warm, and Jerrica felt the heat from his hand travel up her arm, over her neck, across her cheek. Suddenly her whole body was a tinderbox, and she felt feverish. The world tipped and spun— silver streaks, silver and blue, the shimmer of water as it swirls down the drain, a pinwheel on the wind—and before she knew what was happening, Jerrica leaned forward and pressed her lips against his.

She kissed him with a ferocity that took Sanjay by surprise, made him catch his breath. Her fingers raked his hair, and he was disturbed by the thrill that went through his body as her other hand touched his neck.

Sanjay knew that he should stop her. It was more than wrong to lead Jerrica on. But he needed her help. And he wasn't sure that he *wanted* her to stop.

Jerrica pulled away, looked at him with those same bottle-green eyes. But her expression had shifted in a way that Sanjay couldn't quite define. "It's all right," he said, although he wasn't sure whether he was saying it to Jerrica or to himself.

They were quiet for a long moment, and Jerrica did her best to focus on her breathing. She turned toward the lake and listened to the breath puff from her nostrils as she shook her head slowly, trying to clear the silvery blue kaleidoscope from her mind. She had known for weeks that this was coming. But when Kat had joined them at the casino, Jerrica had felt the silvery shape lose form, the way a piece of skywriting dissipates on the wind. Now it was back . . .

"Jerrica," Sanjay said after a moment, "I came here because I needed to talk to you about something."

Jerrica nodded slightly, still half lost in her kaleidoscope.

"I was hoping that you might . . ." Sanjay cleared his throat, feeling suddenly ridiculous. But the stakes were too high. "Do you remember saying that you didn't want to play roulette anymore?"

"I remember."

"Jerrica." Reaching out, he touched her chin. She turned away for a moment, then looked up at him. Sanjay had to resist the urge to squirm under her gaze. "I want you to apply the Principles again."

Jerrica shook her head. "No."

"Why not?"

Before her, the silver image blurred and shifted. She felt tears at the edges of her lower lids and knew they were about to spill over. "I just can't," she whispered. How could she explain that she didn't want to face the casinos—the vivid kaleidoscopes, the whirling patterns—if she couldn't even predict when Sanjay was going to get hurt? She just couldn't face it. *I can't control anything, can't help anyone. The numbers ... what use are they?*

"Jerrica." Sanjay ran his fingertips down the length of Jerrica's right arm, sending a shiver through her. "Jerrica—what if I told you I needed you?"

She looked at him sharply.

"I'm in trouble," he said simply.

Jerrica turned back to the lake. The wind had picked up slightly, and small ripples were moving across the water. Sanjay remembered what she had said about patterns. Patterns in clouds, patterns in sand ...

"I'm begging you, Jerrica," Sanjay said. "Just once more. I hate to ask you, but there's no one else—"

"I said, I don't want to." She felt dizzy and sick; she could hardly breathe.

"Jerrica." He pulled her close, placing his lips against her hair.

"I don't want anyone to get hurt." Her face was pressed against his blue button-down shirt. She breathed in the smell of it, clean and fresh.

"But I'm not hurt," Sanjay replied. "I'm fine."

"It could have been worse, Sanjay," Jerrica whispered into his chest.

"I understand." His voice was a whisper, and he ran his hand up and down her back, rhythmically. He was surprised at how small and light her bones were—like a little bird's. "But I thought you were so close to figuring out those, uh, Principles, Jerrica," he said after a moment.

She tilted her head to look up into his face. "I thought I was."

"Then you shouldn't give up now." He looked down at her, his dark eyes soft. "Just try it once more. Why not?" A wave of dizziness shot through Sanjay, and he realized that his body was coursing with adrenaline.

He smiled at her. It was a look that took hold of her throat, made her catch her breath. *Sanjay needs you,* she told herself. *He admits it.* The loneliness that had bloomed in her chest shriveled slightly, pulled back. "This Thursday," she said at last. "Early evening," she added, remembering her weekly appointment with Janet.

Sanjay nodded. "Good, Jerrica. That's really good."

They walked out of the park and back toward Jerrica's cold house.

The short walk over seemed like a long walk back. "Well," Sanjay said when they finally reached her front door.

But Jerrica quickly opened the door and vanished inside. Sanjay found himself staring at the dark wooden door for a moment. When he turned around, he saw that the light had diminished and the thin strips of cloud had disappeared.

"**d**ammit," Kat said when she put her eye to the peephole. She wondered if she could dart back to her room and hide under the covers. But she'd have to face him sooner or later. She flipped the new deadbolt Trish had installed when she broke up with her last boyfriend and stepped aside so that Mike could enter.

"Hey, sweetness," he said. Even in the low light, Kat could see the hard gleam of his eyes.

"Hey, Mike," Kat said.

"It looks like things have cooled off," he said. He tried to smile, but it looked like a wince. "I need my stuff now."

Kat pressed her lips together. "Mike . . ." Her eyes slipped over the worn brown couch at the center of the living room. "What would you say if I told you that I needed to borrow some of that money?"

"How much?"

"A thousand?"

"A thousand." Mike's eyebrows arched in surprise. "That's a serious chunk."

"I would get it back to you in two days."

"Now I'm really curious." Mike dropped onto the couch, his long legs extended in front of him.

Kat perched beside him, her spine rigid. "Look, Mike, I—" Kat cleared her throat. "I know someone." And then Kat explained all about Jerrica; told him about the money she had won, about getting comped at the hotel. "We're gonna make a lot of money, fast."

"What do you need a lot of money for, Kat?" Mike asked.

Kat stood up. "Never mind. This is stupid."

"Hey."

She felt his hand brushing her leg, saw his hard eyes staring up at her. "It's okay," Mike said. "You don't have to tell me everything."

"So can I borrow the money?"

"I don't know." Mike traced his finger in a circle on the back of Kat's leg, making her shiver. "Psychic cards? Sounds like bullshit."

"It isn't."

Mike looked at her, studying her face. "If you're telling the truth, I might be interested in taking a cut."

As she looked at Mike, she caught a whiff of memory. Mike in the seventh grade, riding his bike at breakneck speed, tearing around the apartment complex where Kat and her mother lived. His friend Malik standing on the rear wheel's pegs, and Mike's hair—it was shorter then, with only a long hank at the back—fluttering in the breeze. *That was only five years ago*, Kat realized, and the thought hit her with sickening intensity. They had both changed so much in only five years . . .

"You can borrow the money," Mike said. "But I want to keep my eye on it. I'll get it to you later."

"Okay."

"What about the other stuff?" Mike asked.

"I have it."

"I'll need it back."

"All right," she said, and started down the hallway to her room.

***

Jerrica was tired of the white box, of the pretty plants, of the fabric art; tired of Janet and her tailored casual wardrobe, her endless selection of glasses with elegant boxy frames. She couldn't think here. There were no answers here; of that Jerrica was certain.

"Jerrica, I got a call from your father yesterday," Janet said.

Jerrica felt acid churn at the base of her stomach. "And?"

"And he wanted to know why I didn't bill him for three sessions."

The silence between them was like an animal crouching in the corner, waiting to pounce. Jerrica looked out the window. She started listing prime numbers, waiting to see if she could feel the familiar drop that let her know what was going to happen . . .

"I explained to him that you had told me that you were going to be out of town on those days," Janet said, yanking Jerrica from her list, thrusting her back into the white office. "Would you care to tell me where you were?"

Jerrica shifted on the couch. "I've been working on a project."

"What kind of project?" Janet's voice was so crisp that Jerrica could hear both the *c* and the *t* punctuating the end of her question.

"A math project," Jerrica explained. "It's an independent study. It's crazy complicated, and I've been needing the extra time to get it done. It's really interesting—it's about probability . . ." Her words were tumbling out now, and Jerrica felt the excitement burbling up from the bottom of her chest. It wasn't easy for her to stop herself from telling Janet everything, but what she had done was illegal; Janet would disapprove, and might even tell her father. "Anyway," Jerrica concluded, forcing herself to use a calm, even tone, "it's more complicated than I thought it would be. I just needed some more study time."

"Why not tell your father about this . . . project?"

Jerrica deflected the question. "Angela really thinks I should see you twice a week."

"And why do you think she wants that?"

Jerrica didn't even bother replying.

"Jerrica . . ." Janet slipped off her glasses—the frames were red today, to match her red shoes and crimson nails—and pressed her thumb and forefinger against the bridge of her nose. "I want to ask you a question, and I want you to answer me truthfully."

"Okay." Jerrica narrowed her eyes, feeling wary.

The therapist replaced her eyeglasses and gazed at Jerrica steadily. "Have you been taking your medication, Jerrica?"

"Of course." She hadn't taken a pill in weeks. And she hadn't missed them. The sluggishness, the memory lapses—all of that had gone away when she stopped. She had never felt better.

"I'm worried about you." Janet's small fingers covered her mouth. Her lips were turned down, and creases reached toward her chin. "After all, your mother—"

"I'm fine," Jerrica said quickly, so that Janet wouldn't have to finish the sentence. She didn't want to hear the word "suicide."

Her mother had died in a car accident. But the bigger truth was that her mother had been driving in the wrong direction on the interstate, her body full of the pills the doctor had prescribed to help her sleep. Jerrica still remembered the grim look on the police officer's face when she answered the door, the odd set of his lips when he asked if her father was at home. She remembered the four long days and nights spent in the hospital before an end that wasn't merciful—not at all, not for anyone. Her sister had died three months earlier, in the same damn hospital.

Janet knew all this. Jerrica knew it. That was no reason to talk about it.

*She really does look worried,* Jerrica thought. She experienced an eerie feeling of warmth. It surprised her how good it felt to have someone care. "Don't worry," Jerrica said at last. "Really."

Janet shook her head. "I'm trusting you."

"I'm not a threat to myself or others," Jerrica said, making a cross over her heart.

"Don't joke, Jerrica."

"I'm not." She was a little taken aback because, of course, she had been joking. "Everything's fine, I swear. I promise not to skip any more sessions, okay?"

Janet glanced down at her leather-bound calendar. *Three hundred sixty-five days. So close to the three hundred sixty degrees of a circle . . .*

"You'll tell me?" Janet said at last. Her face was full of doubt. And beneath that, fear. "You'll tell me if you think there's a danger . . ."

Jerrica felt a wave of sympathy for her. "I guess," she said. "I mean, I will. Of course."

\*\*\*

"What's he doing here?" Sanjay asked as he pulled neatly between the white lines. He and Kat were five minutes late. Jerrica would already be inside, waiting.

Mike was standing nearby. He looked surprisingly elegant in a pair of dark jeans, a black T-shirt, and an olive suede jacket.

"He's meeting us." Kat's voice was flat. "We're using his money—he's taking a cut."

Sanjay yanked the handle and stepped out of the car. Quickly,

Kat slid out and slammed the door shut behind her. Her heels make a hollow *pock, pock, pock* sound against the concrete as she hurried after him.

The side of Mike's mouth twisted up into a half smile. "Well, hello there, San-jay," he said.

Sanjay nodded slightly. "Mike."

Mike's eyes flicked to the ugly stitches at the side of Sanjay's face. "I see you've been making new friends."

Sanjay let the comment float away—imagined it fluttering three stories down to street level. They were standing in a parking garage, near the rear entrance to the Future Galaxy, and tourists were streaming past. It wasn't worth making a scene.

"Did you bring the money?" Kat asked.

Mike's smirk didn't fade as he rested his gaze on her face. "Of course." He held out an elbow in a courtly gesture. "Shall we?"

"You can't go in with her," Sanjay said.

Mike's eyes were cold. "Like hell I can't."

"Seriously, Mike," Kat snapped. "Jerrica won't play if you're there."

Mike tossed his shaggy golden hair out of his eyes. "If there isn't any money, she *can't* play," he retorted, narrowing his eyes. The look reminded Kat of the lions they kept at Phantasy—all that coiled, dangerous power.

Kat shook her head. "She's not going to go for it. She's all about flying below the radar."

"Listen—this is *my* money we're talking about." Mike gripped her arm, his strong fingers sinking into her flesh. "I'm going in there."

"Let go of her," Sanjay warned him.

Mike released Kat suddenly, sending her stumbling backward. Her arm throbbed where he had gripped it. *What made me think this was a good idea?* she wondered wildly. *What the hell am I doing?* "You know what? Let's forget the whole thing." She turned back toward Sanjay's car.

"No, Kat—wait." This was Sanjay's voice. His eyes shot from Kat to Mike as he ran a hand through his hair. "It'll be okay," he said. "Just as long as he doesn't bet."

Kat saw the steel in Mike's face, and for a moment she wasn't sure that Mike would agree to this. "Just stand there with me," she said. "Just watch." She heard the pleading in her voice, and it made her sick.

"Fine," he spat. He turned his back on her and walked toward the casino.

"I'll be out here," Sanjay told her. He didn't dare set foot inside.

Kat touched his shoulder lightly, then turned to follow Mike.

***

Jerrica drew her fingers across the green felt, feeling the gentle scratch of the painted number. She could feel those golden eyes on her, but she tried to ignore them. Kat's friend made her uncomfortable. She wanted to help Sanjay, but it was hard to shake the feeling of disquiet that had settled into her stomach. Janet had unnerved her that afternoon. Jerrica craved the comfort of her numbers . . .

Kat placed her bets and the white ball rolled and bounced. Another win—on the split for Jerrica, on the corner for Kat.

Mike put a hand on Kat's waist. Jerrica could sense his impatience from across the table. He didn't understand why she didn't put it all down on one number—take the money and run. Jerrica wondered if Kat had explained the process to him—if she had told him that they would win slowly, cash out, and then move on.

"Seventeen is the winner," the croupier announced. "Number seventeen."

Jerrica pursed her lips. She had been playing cards in her room for twenty-four hours straight, turning over card after card until she fell asleep over them. Then she would snap out of her doze, make a note in her notebook, and begin turning cards again. At first she had only been trying to feel the drop, to get to the place where she could predict the cards. But then, after a while, she had started changing the outcomes.

First the colors came to her and she saw a five of diamonds. She held that image in her mind, held it as clear as she could for a moment—and then, slowly, watched the colors shift. She turned them herself, letting the kaleidoscope unfurl, changing the image to a jack of spades.

And when she drew the next card, there it was.

Now a yellow starburst leaped into her mind. At the center, a blue swirl tipped with deep pinkish gold, and at the edges, a deep blue, almost black—the black of space, of a void; the emptiness of a black hole, sucking, yearning, pulling her in, drawing her into its impossible gravity . . .

Delicately, Jerrica drew her thumb across the double zero.

Kat reached over to put her chips on the zero–double zero split, but a large hand closed over hers, guiding her chips to the double zero.

Mike grinned down at Kat. "Let's bet a little bigger, honey," he said, reaching for a larger stack of her chips. "Let's take a risk."

Kat's voice disappeared. She wanted to say no, but all she could do was watch as Mike slipped her chips to the double zero.

"Sir?" The croupier's voice was stern as he eyed Mike coldly. He nodded at Kat. "The lady must place the bet."

This was her chance. But Mike's arm was around her waist, pinning her against the table. "It's all right," she croaked to the croupier, who nodded.

The croupier spun the wheel, and the white ball began its familiar dance. Kat didn't dare look up at Jerrica's eyes, which burned with twin green flames. This was Kat's accidental win all over again. She was surprised that Jerrica hadn't already stalked out—maybe she thought it would look too strange to abandon her bet?

Skip, bounce, drop.

"The winner is number twenty-four," the croupier announced. "Number twenty-four."

"Shit," Kat said under her breath. She stared at the small pocket that held the marble, fighting the urge to tell the croupier that he wasn't right, that something had gone wrong, that the ball wasn't where it belonged. Double zero. It belonged on double zero!

She looked up in time to see Jerrica walking away from the table, blending into the crowd as it swirled back and forth under the exit signs. The pressure against her waist lifted, and in the next confused second she saw that Mike was hurrying after Jerrica.

"Let's go," he whispered, not breaking his stride, and Kat tripped after him, nearly slamming into a gray-haired man in a green baseball cap.

"Watch it!" the man's wife hollered, covering Kat's hurried apology.

As Kat pushed open the casino's glass door—smudged from the thousands of fingers that had touched it over the course of the last three hours—she found herself standing at the edge of a line of people waiting for taxis. To her left, Mike had broken into a run, and Kat hurried after him as well as she could in her heels. The concrete sloped down, shooting pain through her knees at every step.

Sanjay hurried to her side. "I just saw Jerrica—"

"Come on," Kat said, dragging him by the arm.

Jerrica had rounded the corner of the twisted parking garage and was nearing a concrete box—an elevator bank with windows on one side. Her car was in a lot two casinos over. Not far. She had never felt such an urge to drive, to feel the power of the machine under her body—

"Hey!" Mike called, and when Jerrica didn't turn around or slow down, he tried again—louder. "Hey!" He grabbed her arm just as she stepped into the elevator bank.

The pain was a shock to Jerrica, as was the sharp-featured face that appeared almost right up against her own. She wanted to tell this person—Kat had said his name was Mike—that there was a stray eyelash right below his golden right eye, but before she could get out the words, Mike snarled, "What the fuck was that?"

"What?"

Mike shoved her against a concrete wall painted a slick, wet-looking beige. Institutional beige. Jerrica remembered it from the hospital. She knew that it was strange that she was paying more attention to the paint than to the thudding noise her skull had just made against the wall, but there it was.

"Double zero, bitch. What the fuck?"

Jerrica shook her head. "I don't know." The problem with beige paint, she now realized, was that it showed black scratches and dings—it somehow always seemed to look dirty and old.

"You just lost a thousand dollars in there." The tip of his nose was almost touching hers, and she could feel the warmth of his breath on her face. "Go get it back."

Jerrica shook her head. "You're the one who lost it."

"How am I supposed to get it back?"

Sanjay flung open the glass door. "Whoa, whoa, whoa!" His black eyes were huge.

"Jesus, Mike," Kat breathed as she stepped into the tiny cube behind Sanjay. She sucked air through her nostrils. "What are you doing? Let her go."

"Not until I get my money. This little rich girl is taking me to an ATM."

"Look, man, I need money, too—okay?"

"I don't give a shit about you."

"I don't give a shit about you, either," Sanjay shot back. "But we're in the same boat, all right?"

"Fuck we are. You don't know the guys I'm dealing with."

"The number should have come up." Jerrica's eyes were locked on Sanjay's face, but he could tell she wasn't seeing him. "I don't know why it didn't come up."

"I can't believe I bought this psychic card crap," Mike said.

"It's not crap," Jerrica insisted. "It's a system—I just haven't worked it out perfectly yet . . ."

"Maybe the wheel was rigged . . ."

"Jerrica—what happened?" Sanjay asked. "Was it a pale number?" She had told him that sometimes the visions were weak and that was when the numbers were unreliable.

"No." Her eyes narrowed. "I'm telling you, it should have come up."

"She don't have a system, man," Mike said. "It's all bullshit."

"Show him the notebook, Jerrica," Sanjay said. "Show him."

Jerrica hesitated.

"Jerrica, you have to," Sanjay said quietly. "Please."

Slowly, Jerrica reached into her messenger bag. She pulled out the battered black-and-white notebook.

"It's all in there," Sanjay said. "How she does it—everything."

Mike grabbed the notebook from her hands and opened it to the first page. Scanned it. Flipped it. Scanned the next. Flip. Flip. Flip. "Holy shit," he said after a moment. He looked up at Sanjay, his eyes narrow. "Have you seen this thing?"

"No, I—"

Mike turned it around for Sanjay to see. He turned a page, then turned another.

"Oh my God," Kat whispered.

Sanjay stared at Jerrica. "What's this?" he asked.

Jerrica's eyes were watching the ceiling; she looked like a Catholic saint. "They're formulas."

"This is nothing but a bunch of goddamn swirls!" Mike flung the notebook at her. "These aren't even numbers!"

Jerrica didn't respond. The notebook bounced off her chest and fell to the floor like a dead thing. The page facing her was a number sixteen—a bold geometric kaleidoscope that Jerrica had drawn in intricate detail. It was a complicated number, full of tiny slivers of color . . .

"It isn't real?" Kat felt ill. And she felt sorry for Jerrica. *She isn't well,* Kat thought, noting Jerrica's pallor, her tired eyes. *Why didn't I see it before?*

"No—it has to be." Sanjay reached for the notebook. He flipped through it but dropped it back where it was. "Jerrica?"

*He believed in me. How can he doubt me now?* "The universe has an order," Jerrica insisted. "I can predict things!"

"The hell you can!" The anger exploded out of Sanjay as the reality of his situation settled around him. "Are you telling me we've been relying on *that*?" He pointed to the notebook. "You're crazy!"

"You've seen it," Jerrica insisted. "You've all seen it." She felt his anger like an arrow in her chest. "Sanjay?" She reached for Sanjay's arm, but he shook her off.

"Get away from me."

Jerrica felt a scream rising in her throat. "Look at me," she begged, but he wouldn't.

"It's okay, Jerrica," Kat said in a low voice.

Jerrica's eyes latched onto hers. "Kat, you've seen it."

"I—" Kat bit her lip. She didn't know what to think.

"You still believe in me," Jerrica whispered.

Mike glared at her. "You are completely insane."

"Don't say that!" Jerrica shouted. The sound of her own voice actually shocked her, vibrating through her chest. "I'm telling you, the wheel must have been rigged! It should have been double zero!"

"What now?" Sanjay asked, not even looking in her direction. *I can't believe I bought this bullshit*, he said to himself. Every scrap of tenderness he'd felt for Jerrica stabbed at him, a thousand needles. *I should have known.*

Kat watched Jerrica's eyes, hesitating. She was staring at Sanjay, hurt etched into her features. *She loves him*, Kat realized, her heart ripping slightly, as if it were made of tissue paper.

"I want my money," Mike snarled, taking a step toward Jerrica.

"Well, you can't have it," Kat snapped, moving between them. "So back off."

"But—"

"I said, *back off.*" Kat felt the adrenaline surging through her body, making her feel dense, as if she were made of iron or lead. "You'll get the money—but not right now, all right? For God's sake, give the girl some space!"

"Okay, okay." Mike held up his hands and stepped away from Jerrica.

It was with a pleasant little jolt that Kat realized that he was actually afraid of her at that moment.

He seemed to realize it, too. "I'm holding you responsible," he added weakly, pointing at Kat.

"Fine," she told him. But she held his eye for an extra beat to remind him that she knew his secrets. There was power in that, and she felt it.

He seemed to get the message. "Okay." He sighed, deflating a little.

"Sanjay?" Jerrica called, but he was already walking away, toward his car. He was simply leaving her there with the notebook at her feet, leaving her feeling more alone than she had before she began feeling her way into the Principles. "Sanjay?"

He didn't look back.

*Everything is connected.* That was what Jerrica had been trying to prove. But in the end, things hadn't been connected at all. The reason the Principles could never be perfect was because you could never live in a perfectly controlled world.

Jerrica felt something soft at her elbow. It was Kat's fingertip. "It's okay," Kat whispered in her ear.

"No," Jerrica replied, "it isn't."

She had to accept this fact—there was no way to ever make things right again.

K at saw Sanjay sitting on the steps leading to her front door before he saw her. She thought about running away, but her feet carried her forward. Sanjay looked up. He stood and waited for her to open the door.

Trish skimped on most things, but not on the air-conditioning. They walked into a cool blast of comfort.

"Damn," Sanjay said as Kat closed the door behind him, "is your aunt storing dead bodies here or something?"

Kat didn't laugh. "Where've you been?"

"I'm not going back to school," Sanjay muttered, flopping on the worn brown couch. His long limbs splayed everywhere. For a moment, he seemed to consider picking up the pile of cards that Lala had left on the coffee table, but he thought better of it and grabbed an orange pillow instead, hugging it to his stomach.

"Never?"

"I'll just get a GED."

Kat perched on the chair opposite him. "What does your dad think?"

"No idea." Sanjay punched the pillow, sending it back into its corner of the couch. "We haven't exactly been having father-son bonding chats, you know?"

"But isn't he—"

Sanjay ran his hands through his hair. "Yeah, he's letting me work at the store to pay it off." He had never seen his father so furious and disappointed. His normally opinionated father hadn't said a word to him in days.

Sanjay's miserable look sent an angry flare through Kat. His father *loved* him, had forgiven him, and he didn't even seem to realize it. *God*, Kat thought, *I'd give anything to have a father like that.* "So what are you doing here, Sanjay?"

Sanjay noticed the edge in her voice, but decided to ignore it. He cleared his throat. "What happened with Mike?"

Kat shook her head. "I'm pulling extra hours at the shoe store. I told him I'd get him the money—it just may take some time."

"That's messed up."

"It's what happens when you don't have a daddy around to save your ass."

The words hit Sanjay like a punch to the gut. *She doesn't want me here*, he realized. He hadn't—not until that moment—allowed himself to believe anything but that Kat would be glad to see him after an absence of eight days. He hadn't returned her text messages or calls, true, but he had been thinking of her. Didn't that count for anything? "You know what?" Sanjay stood up. "I think I'll take off." He hesitated at the door, unsure of what to say. "Maybe I'll see you around?" is what he settled on.

"Maybe." Kat didn't lift herself out of her chair until she heard the door click behind him. She picked up the mail that Trish had placed in a basket on a narrow wooden table behind the couch. At the bottom was a crumpled yellow padded envelope. *K. Phelps*, it read. There was no address. Someone had dropped it off by hand.

*Weird*, Kat thought as she collapsed on the couch. Reaching in, she pulled out the contents of the envelope. "Oh my God," she whispered.

Bills. Hundred-dollar bills. Her hands trembled. *There must be five thousand dollars here.*

On top of the stack, a Post-it note. *One last bet*, it read. *J.*

*One last bet—and it had paid off.*

So maybe Jerrica had been right after all. Maybe she wasn't crazy. She was just . . . whatever she was.

*But why me?*

*Maybe because you're the only one who didn't turn on her,* whispered a voice.

So there it was. She had the money. Enough to pay off Mike and . . .

*Enough to run . . .*

"Are we going to live with Mama again?" Lala had asked three nights ago, when Kat told her about the parole hearing. Her eyes were bright.

"Why?" Kat asked. "Do you miss her?"

Lala thought for a moment. She looked up at Kat but didn't reply. Kat wondered if she was remembering the time Julia had left them sitting in a car for ten hours. Lala was only four, and Kat had been eleven. They had sat there overnight, with the doors locked tight. Kat hadn't dared get out of the car to go get help. She kept telling herself that her mother would be back soon, be back any minute . . .

And now, here it was—she had the money. She could just take Lala and start over . . .

But now that she was faced with a choice, the idea seemed childish, impossible. *Where am I going to go? What kind of job can I get?* And then a new thought: *Isn't it kidnapping to run with Lala?* The money felt hot in her hands; she closed her eyes to shut out the sick feeling in her stomach.

Her mother's parole hearing was in three days, and if Julia wanted custody, she needed Kat to lie. Again. To say that Julia was a kind, caring, responsible mother. To forget everything else.

*Why are these my choices?*

Opening her eyes, she spotted Lala's red-backed Bicycle cards. Kat picked up the top card. Nine of hearts. *What does this mean? Anything?*

Kat held the card over the pile and let it drop.

At that moment, there was a jingling at the door, a sound like distant bells. Then the deadbolt flipped and the door swung open. Kat shoved the money back into the envelope and under a cushion as Trish stepped inside. When she saw Kat, her exhausted face rearranged itself into a smile. "Hey," Trish said.

That voice. It was the same as Julia's.

*But Trish isn't Julia,* Kat thought.

"Is everything okay?" Trish asked as she placed her purse on the nicked-up white side table by the door. She kicked off her heels and padded over in her stockings to sit on the couch beside Kat.

"Trish," Kat said slowly, "there's something I wanted to talk to you about."

"Anything," Trish said. Reaching out, she took Kat's hand.

Kat took a deep breath. Then another. Trish gave her fingers an encouraging squeeze.

Kat looked at her aunt's face—her mottled skin, the worry lines on her forehead. Nothing had been easy for Trish, and it showed. There was something comforting about that. Trish wasn't afraid of things just because they were hard.

"Trish, what if I didn't testify at my mother's parole hearing?"

Trish leaned back against a couch pillow, keeping her even glance on Kat's face. "Well, I guess she may not get out..." Trish cleared her throat. "Kat—I've spoken with your mother. No matter what happens, I think it might be best if you stayed with me for a while. I don't know if your mother..."

Kat nodded slowly, but her heart thrummed wildly. This was what she had wanted all along—to stay with her aunt. For Lala to stay here. "For how long?"

"I don't know." Trish cocked her head, studying Kat's face. A long moment passed between them. "Is there something you want to tell me?"

Kat cleared her throat and took yet another deep breath. She drew the air deep into her lungs, then let it out in a long, even stream. She looked at her aunt, whose face said, *It's okay.*

She remembered the power of saying no to Mike, how good it felt to protect Jerrica. *And isn't that what I'm doing now—protecting Lala? If I tell Trish the truth about Julia, she'll let us stay. She has to.*

Kat knew that telling the truth was a risk. *But everything's a risk. Look at Jerrica—knowing what was supposed to happen hadn't helped her.*

*All I have to do is decide which risk to take.*

Her aunt actually seemed like a pretty good bet.

"Yes," Kat said at last. "There's something I want to tell you."

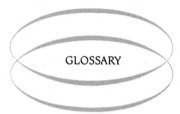

GLOSSARY

**action:** A bet of any kind. To take action is to accept bets, acting as a bookie.

**advantaged player:** A bettor with an edge over the casino—in blackjack, players who can count cards are considered advantaged.

**all in:** Having bet the remainder of your funds.

**blind:** A mandatory bet made before the cards are dealt.

**cage:** The cashier area in a casino.

**corner:** In roulette, a bet laid on the intersection of four numbers, covering all four at once.

**counting cards:** A method of memorizing and keeping track of which cards have been played in order to gauge whether the remaining cards might favor the player(s) or dealer.

**double blind:** The two bets made before the cards are dealt. The first bet is usually known as the small blind, made by the player to the left of the dealer. The second bet is usually known as the big blind. Often twice the amount of the small blind, this bet is made by the player two seats to the left of the dealer.

**double-down:** In blackjack, to double the size of one's original bet before taking a final card.

**drop:** The term used in casinos for the gross amount wagered at the tables.

**flop:** In the poker game called Texas Hold 'Em, the first three cards that are revealed. These are communal cards—they are shared by all players.

**fold:** To forfeit one's hand.

**full house:** A hand containing three cards of one rank and two of another. For example, a hand containing three sevens and a pair of fives.

**knock:** To rap one's knuckles on the table indicating that one is taking a pass on the current bet in a hand of poker. The player can later choose to match the bet, raise, or fold.

**raise:** To increase the amount of money bet in a hand of poker.

**river:** In Texas Hold 'Em, the final card dealt.

**royal flush:** In poker, a hand consisting of a ten, jack, queen, king, and ace, all of the same suit. This hand has the highest value, beating all others.

**see:** To match a previously made bet without raising it.

**shoe:** A dispenser holding several decks of cards.

**split:** In roulette, a bet laid on the line between two numbers, covering both at once.

**stay:** To match an existing bet in a hand of poker.

**straight up:** In roulette, a bet on a single number.

**tell:** A (usually unconscious) gesture or behavior that reveals something about a player's hand or style of play.

**Texas Hold 'Em:** The most popular form of poker played in American casinos. A player may use any combination of five communal cards and his or her own two cards to make a standard poker hand.

**turn:** In Texas Hold 'Em, the fourth card dealt.

## SPECIAL THANKS

Special thanks to Gary L. Powell for his expertise in casino surveillance and security and to Marlene Warner of the Massachusetts Council on Compulsive Gambling for sharing her thoughts on teen gambling. Heartfelt thanks to my editor, Cecile Goyette, for never losing patience with this book, and to my agent, Rosemary Stimola, for her unflagging support. Love and gratitude to my family, especially my husband, who read and reread several drafts of this book. Thanks to Ellen Wittlinger, Nancy Werlin, and Pat Lowery Collins for their insight into the manuscript, and to Miliann Kang and Helen Perelman for their enthusiasm for this project.